As you wade into the tapestry of the imagination, explore the essence of the human spirit on its enduring adventure with the bow and arrow.

Fireside Tales awaits you.

Watch out for stray sparks!

BOWHUNTING FIRESIDE TALES

DAN BERTALAN

Dan Bertalan

Envisage Unlimited Press East Lansing, Michigan

First Printed 1994

10 9 8 7 6 5 4 3 2 1

Manufactured in the United States of America.

Library of Congress Catalog Card Number: 94-70353

ISBN 0-9623955-3-6

Envisage Unlimited Press
P.O. Box 777
East Lansing, Michigan 48826
517-834-2276

PUBLISHER'S NOTE
This is a work of fiction. Names, characters, places, and incidents either are the product of the author's imagination or are used fictitiously, and any resemblance to actual persons, living or dead, events, or locales is entirely coincidental.

Table of Contents

ACKNOWLEDGMENTS

I am grateful to Mark Woodbury and Will Wuerthele
for their editorial assistance.

This book is dedicated to those
not paying attention — daydreamers.

INTRODUCTION

Except for Chapter 1, *The Spirit Lives*, the following collection of bowhunting stories is a journey into the imagination. The remaining fictional chapters use the arenas of humor, horror, myth, and nostalgia to dredge up a host of thoughts and emotions about how the human spirit is intertwined with bowhunting.

Besides hopefully being entertaining, each story carries a message or theme. Some are obvious while others work like a brewing pot of coffee, simmering in the back of the mind and eventually finding its own richness and flavor.

The title, *Fireside Tales*, reflects the presence of a fire of some sort in many of the tales. The obvious ones are campfires, a few others are wood stoves, gas ranges, porch lights, or even the brief flicker of an idea or the fiery twinkle in an eye. Another aspect of *Fireside Tales* is that the stories are meant to be enjoyed near a fireside — whether alone at home or in hunting camp with a troop of buddies.

So kick back, throw another log on the fire or cuddle near a lamp with a steaming cup of brew, and wade into the tapestry of the mind. Enjoy the ride, watch out for stray sparks, and savor the essence of the human spirit on its enduring adventure with the bow and arrow.

PRESERVING THE SPIRIT

I quit deer hunting early this evening, shooting my practice arrow into the dirt long before last light. I knew the deer would spook at the noise. I smiled when they did. Watching their tails flag though the woods lifted my spirit, their graceful bounds carrying a piece of my soul into the shadows. At times the wonder of life going on tastes so much sweeter than the bitter tinge of ending it.

Though killing marks the end of the hunt, it has always been an internal battle. Forces of love, logic, and instinct clash between my heart and the hunter lurking in my soul. It's forever a struggle. But more so lately.

As a bowhunter the struggle usually wins out to the rush of adrenaline. The arrow sings on its way without remorse — at least until I look into the glazed eyes and feel the fleeting warmth. Then the bittersweetness of the harvest takes over. It lingers for a long time, yet I know the hunter within will surface again. He always does. Almost always.

Three years ago the hunter failed to come out. That day I wanted to kill a whitetail. I knew I should. Without question, it was the right thing to do. Still I couldn't. Maybe it was that I had a gun in my hands instead of a bow. But that shouldn't have mattered. I wasn't killing for the climax of a hunt or for meat. I'd convinced myself I was killing for mercy. I was going to shoot a crippled doe.

I first saw her in January that year. I was working at my desk, writing some hunting story I suppose, when I noticed a flicker out the window; deer. A handful of them loped across the field behind the house and paused in the aspens to nibble a few shoots. Just as I turned back to my work I caught sight of another form emerging from the woods — a loner, trying to catch up.

I knew something was wrong the moment I saw her. Maybe it was the way she came bucking across the snow in short jerky strides. Then she fell. Snow sprayed as her face plowed through the weeds.

I grabbed my binoculars for a closer look. Part of me wished I hadn't. She righted herself like a beached seal, revealing her desperate struggle. Her right leg hung like a twisted piece of rope. Torn flesh and knotted cartilage somehow held the mess together as she again lunged forward. The leg flipped sickly around and battered her side as it caught some brush.

The pain in her haggard face and her struggle to carry on despite it showed all too plainly. Part of her wanted to stop, to give up the hopeless fight. She wanted to rid herself of the now worthless leg and the whole withering body that would soon die to the rip of running dogs or pang of starvation. The plumes of frosted breath, the heaving ribs, the dangling tongue, the sides drawn and taut, all said she wouldn't make it. They also cried for mercy.

Maybe it had been a car, maybe dogs, probably a page-wire fence; most certainly some doings of man. The only thing I knew for sure was that a man must end it. I knew by man's written rules it was wrong. But a deeper sense pleaded that rules weren't written for this. I grabbed my .22 rifle.

I paused as she finally caught up to the herd, somehow hoping the deer could help their wounded. Foolish notion. Instead of mercy she was greeted with flailing hooves, driven back by two lead does. They wanted no part of her fleshy smell. She was dog bait, a cripple. The pain and confusion in her eyes made me turn away. I headed for the door.

I slipped into the woods as most of the deer melted into the timber. The cripple, still catching her breath and confused, wavered on her one good front leg in the morning stillness.

I chambered a hollow-point. A dozen more waited behind it. Poor bullets for killing deer but I knew it would take what little thread of life remained in her. At forty yards I raised the rifle. She caught my movement and looked up as I fought to steady the gun. I met her stare over the sights. She had the same look of internal struggle that gripped me. Part of her wanted to die, yet somewhere behind the pain, a bigger part urged her to live. I swallowed hard, then lowered the gun. I couldn't.

Only seconds before I'd had so many reasons to kill her, so many good reasons backed by mercy and fairness in a setting that was so unmerciful and unfair. I turned and walked away. Fate had brought her this far. Fate would have to claim her. I had failed to do what was right. I had failed to do what was wrong.

That winter the snows piled and the wind sliced across the landscape. It got bitchly cold. I knew winter's hand had killed her. If not the cold, surely the running dogs had finished the job — tearing the part of her that wanted to live from the struggling mess that had once been a glorious animal. There was no doubt.

Yet somehow she lived.

I saw her again in the spring before green-up. Her once ropy leg now withered tight to her body looking more like a gnarled claw than a leg. Still lagging behind the herd in her choppy strides, she hung on. That once frayed thread of life now stretched as a tight cord. I could see in her face she wasn't about to let go of it either. The ragged circles under her eyes now looked hardened against the pain. Even though the other deer still swiped at her with sharp feet, she hobbled after them, chasing life with a spirit that showed in her struggle.

It seemed less amazing each time I saw her after that. And each time I felt less pity for her plight. Understandably, she had no fawns. Even as summer wore on she never looked healthy, and I was sure she'd wouldn't make it another season, yet somehow she did. And then another.

The next time I saw her up close was late last December after a fresh snow. As I slipped through the maze of powdered branches with bow in hand, I heard the thumping of deer hooves and the unmistakable grunting of a buck.

Out of the whiteness, in her now familiar lurching gait, came the cripple. Hot on her heels followed a rangy six-pointer. He didn't care that she only had three good legs. She smelled right and he wanted her. He harried her for fifteen minutes, once passing within ten yards. I let them flicker by without interrupting the magic of their game. The buck appeared determined, as they always do, but it seemed unlikely he would catch her, and if he did, even more unlikely anything would come of it.

I'd almost forgotten about that snowy day last winter as I went hunting this evening. The first deer to feed in front of me was a pleasant surprise — the cripple. Now seeming like an old friend, a tenacious gripper to life, she fed on the plush rye. Naturally, she grazed alone and didn't stray near the other deer that appeared later.

Then something even more surprising happened. As she hobbled close to the goldenrod at the field's edge, two fawns burst from the cover and trotted up to her. Her tail fluttered as each one nuzzled under her and began nursing. They looked like late fawns by their size, but they were fat and still plenty big enough to make it through the winter. December bred fawns I suppose. Six-pointers can be persistent.

To some, deer look alike. But I swear those fawns wore something special in their high-stepping prance — a spirit that reflected their mother's grit and thirst for life. Like their mom, they also appeared more alert for danger, and ready to someday fight the odds and cheat the hand of death. As the fawns finished their short drink they broke away chasing each other in playful circles, mother's milk dripping from their chins on the green carpet of rye.

The struggle to enjoy hunting got a lot harder this evening. The more precious life appears, the tougher that struggle becomes. It felt good shooting my arrow into the bare ground and letting the trio know that hunters lurk in the woods. I may not hunt deer next year where the cripple lives. One of her fawns may be wearing horns by then.

Her spirit deserves to live on.

I HATE HORSES

I began hating horses when I was four. I was at the playground and one of the older kids coaxed me over to the nearby pasture where a horse stood near the fence. The kid assured me that this horse loved little kids like me. I wasn't much bigger than a grasshopper then and the horse looked every bit as big as the Trojan horse I had seen in a picture book, except this one moved.

The kid gave me an apple and told me to feed it to the horse. But he cautioned me that the horse might choke if I fed it too fast and that I should wrap my fingers around the apple real tight. The horse's eyes widened when he saw the apple and drool started dripping from its mouth.

The last thing I remember seeing clearly was all those giant yellow horse teeth behind those slobbering lips engulf my hands. Then it bit; apple, fingers, all to the core. I screamed like the steam whistle down at the lumber mill and the horse reared wildly, my hands still clenched in its mouth. It seemed astonishing at the time but I guess it wasn't such a feat for a one-ton horse to jerk all thirty pounds of me through two strands of barbed wire, stripping my bib overalls all the way down to my ankles. Then it dropped me on this single piece of wire held up by these shiny things on short posts. I also learned to hate electrical fences that day. But mostly, I hated horses.

I avoided them for years and did a pretty good job all things considered. Oh, I had a few give me the evil eye near the pony ride at the carnival and even had one run me into the mucky lake when I tried fishing from shore in a pasture. They finally caught up to me when I was fifteen and trying to impress a pretty redhead. Like all girls that age she loved horses and wanted to go horseback riding. She obviously didn't know that horses cause more deaths each year than spiders and snakes combined. But I wasn't about to tell her I hated the damn things and mess up my chances of getting my first kiss. So I went riding, or at least tried. The horse won again, this time biting my arm, running me into a thornapple tree and finally bucking me off in front of that pretty redhead. No first kiss that day. Glue. They should all be made into glue.

The decades passed and I stayed clear of horses, but my hate for them still burned. It all seemed innocent enough when my two best buddies asked me to go on a pack-in elk hunt. Man, I loved back packing into remote areas and had always dreamed of bowhunting the west. I jumped at the chance and sent in my $500 deposit pronto. I even bought new boots and a back pack with a fancy frame and camo pack.

Four weeks later they sent me a brochure about the pack-in hunt. I opened it then sank to my knees. There they were in black and white; horses, lots of horses — horses packing in bowhunters, horses packing tents, horses standing in mountain meadows, and horses packing out elk racks. Even in the pictures I could tell they were all just waiting for a horse hater like me to show my face in camp so they could throw me off a mountain or chew me to shreds when no one was looking. Naw, not me. I asked for my deposit back.

"Too Late", the outfitter wrote back. He said that he couldn't refund my deposit because he had already spent it on pasturing and rigging my horse for the pack-in hunt. I wrote back and told him he could sell the damn horse for dog food for all I cared. I just wanted my money back. He must have been a horse lover. He never replied. I never saw my 500 bucks.

I had already scheduled vacation time for the hunt and told all my buddies I was headed for the wild west. So I was determined to salvage some kind of western hunt as long as it didn't involve horses. Fate finally turned her pretty face my way when I heard of one last opening on an antelope hunt in Wyoming. The price was right and I talked to the guy direct and he assured me that I wouldn't have to contend with any horses. Hot damn, I was headed west.

It was still an hour before first light as I neared the water hole the outfitter had shown me the day before. He had to tend to some other hunters in the next county but I told him I could manage by myself. How complicated could sitting in a pit blind be anyway?

Up ahead the water mirrored a million stars glittering overhead. Off to the side sat my pit blind, surrounded by a screen of sage. The outfitter who had leased the hunting rights on this ranch had warned me to check my pit each morning for snakes so I flicked on my flashlight. Suddenly, a terrible roar rose from behind me near the water hole. Startled, I dropped the light into the pit as I spun backward from the attack. I fully expected a bear or lion to hit me full in the chest and braced myself for the impact. But nothing came pounding from the darkness. I listened. I squinted into the gloom.

At first it appeared as only a ripple at the water's edge. Then as my eyes grew more accustomed to the dark, I made out the hideous shape of the thing; a horse stuck in the mud right in front of my blind. I inched closer. It bellowed again, its roar ringing across the prairie. Hell, it was going to scare off half the antelope in Wyoming. I crept closer, whispering quietly to it.

"Now hush, hush. We all have to go someday pal, this water hole ain't such a bad place."

It roared again.

"Come on now, pipe down. At least you ain't going to be dog food or hide glue. With any luck you'll be preserved as a fossil. So count your lucky stars and hush up."

Its roar now held a tone of despair, pleading for me to help. Naw, not me. I hated horses. I walked back to the pit blind and climbed in. Nothing I could do anyway.

An hour later the first wave of antelope came trotting toward the water hole, a huge buck leading the way. Finally, western bowhunting fame was about to be mine. The antelope stiffened at the far crest of the water hole when they spotted the horse. The horse spotted them and bellowed. They were off, a cloud of dust raising in their wake as they sped away across the sage flats.

I scrambled from my blind and stormed down to the horse.

"Now look, you got yourself into this mess. It's not my fault and I can't help you. So do us both a favor and just lie still and keep quiet before, well, before I have to shoot you."

It gave me a snorting plea.

"Listen, I'm not going to warn you again. I'm not a very good shot and it may take several arrows to finish you."

It blinked those big brown eyes at me, apparently seeing through my ruse.

"And my broadheads are dull and rusty too," I threw back as I turned toward the pit. "It'll hurt real bad."

It snorted and whinnied. I climbed into the pit and nocked an arrow. It snorted again. I pointed the bow at it and glared.

Twenty minutes later a lone buck came trotting toward the water. I glared again at the horse and pointed to my broadhead, shook my head, and pressed a finger against my lips. It obviously didn't understand simple sign language. The second it spotted the antelope it began struggling and roaring. The buck bolted across the prairie. I bolted from my blind.

"Okay, that's it. I paid good money for this hunt and I ain't about to let you spoil it anymore."

I scuffed my boot in the dirt. The horse nickered. It must have known there was no way I could bring myself to shoot the helpless thing. I don't hate anything that much, not even horses. I reached out and stroked its muzzle. It made a faint whimpering noise and laid back its ears.

"Alright, how can I help?"

The horse's back legs were mired in the mud all the way to its flanks. It had struggled so long that each leg had made its own giant post hole four feet deep. And from the pile of horse droppings mixed in with the watery mess around its haunches, it must have been there for some time. Its front legs were splayed out on the hard packed mud at the edge of the water, its chest rubbed raw from where it had been struggling to free itself.

"Okay, maybe we can pull you out."

I took off my camo sweater and tied the arms around the horse's neck. I overcame the flashbacks of that horse yanking me through the fence by the hands and let the horse brush my hand with its lips. If I didn't know better I would have admitted it almost felt like a kiss. Naw, not from a horse.

"Alright, on the count of three, I pull, you help. One-two-threeeee..."

I pulled until the arms of my sweater would have fit Michael Jordan. The horse tried to push itself from the mire but its legs trembled like aspen leaves in the wind. It finally fell back on its quivering haunches. I slumped at its side, fingering the ruined sweater; my lucky sweater to boot. A shadow passed over the water hole. We looked up. A pair of vultures flared wide wings on the updrafts. The horse flashed me a worried look.

"Don't panic. This is the only water hole I have to hunt and I'm not about to let your rotting carcass spoil it."

I had heard enough stories about men getting their brains bashed in by a horse's rear hoof but I overcame my fears and waded into the foul slime around the horse's flanks.

"Nice horsey. The only way we're going to get you out of here is to free these back legs. So don't get wild and go kicking my face in. Okay?"

The horse looked back and made a nickering noise. I tried to convince myself it understood and agreed to the bargain. I reached around one of the legs and pulled for all I was worth. With steady tension, its leg slid from the muck. I wallowed my way around to the other leg and repeated the process. With both of its legs free from the holes, I stroked its flank and began to push it up.

"Come on horsey, stand up. You can do it. That's it. You're almost..."

As it stood, my foot slipped forward into the hole and it swallowed my leg like the giant maw of the swamp thing. The instant I fell and stopped pushing, the horse slid backward, its leg sliding into the hole on top of mine, pinning us both in the hole.

At that moment I tried to image a worse place on earth than being trapped under a ton of slimy horse, up to my armpits in mud, the south end of a northbound horse staring me in the face at pointblank range. But I couldn't. God, I hoped its bowels held. What a way to die. We wouldn't even be fit for the vultures. The image of a fused man-horse fossil caused me to wriggle frantically. Anthropologists would never understand. I wiggled some more.

Somehow I managed to free myself and again pull the horse's legs from the holes. This time I crawled around in front of it and grabbed the sweater.

"Okay, bud, this is it. One good yank to stand up and you're free."

I pulled on the sweater and the horse lifted itself on wobbly legs. I was just about to shout with joy when it staggered sideways and both rear legs slipped back into the cavernous holes. It splashed back into the mud with a grunt. Damn. Maybe the vultures would dine after all.

I sank to my knees next to the horse. I looked into its eyes, the last flicker of hope fading, their chestnut pools looking flat with a gaze of acceptance. It looked as if it wanted to cry.

"Come on, stop your pouting. I won't quit if you won't. We've come this far. Let's give it another shot."

The horse sighed and its nose dipped to the mud.

"Fine, be a horse's behind. I'll do it myself. I'm not going to stand around and let you wreck my huntin'."

Covered with mud and slimed horse manure, I wallowed back into the stuff and again pulled the horse's legs from the holes. This time I shoved the horse to the side as much as I could. It didn't resist, it didn't struggle, it just laid there panting, the last of strength fading.

"Come on, this time we'll make it for sure."

Again I pulled on the sweater around its neck while yanking it partly off to the side. The horse didn't budge. I pulled again. Still it didn't have the strength to stand.

"Hey, get with the program. Or do you want to wind up on their menu?" I pointed skyward. The vultures hovered lower. "Their beaks are duller than my broadheads. It's gotta hurt real bad, I mean real bad."

The horse blinked then looked toward the sky. It perked up immediately. I pulled. It pushed. Finally, we both were free.

I slowly led the horse up the bank away from the water. With each step it seemed to rediscover the strength in its wobbly legs. I got to the top near my blind and untied what was left of my lucky sweater from around its neck, the once fine wool now covered with horse hair, mud, and froth.

"There you go," I said stroking its neck. "Now getty-up back to the corral or barn or wherever horses are supposed to live in Wyoming."

The horse stepped forward and nuzzled my hand. Oh boy.

"Yes, you're a nice horsey but you have to leave now. I've got some hunting to finish and I'm sure somebody misses you somewhere. Now beat it. Shoo!"

I tried to wipe the horse dung slime off my pants as best I could with the now worthless sweater then climbed back into my blind. I nocked an arrow and settled back.

"Beat it horse! Off with you."

My new-found friend nickered and edged closer to my blind, squinting its chestnut eyes at me. Before I could grab a stick to slap it on the flank, I noticed dots of white drifting across the prairie. Antelope. Damn, nothing to do but wait now. Maybe the horse will prove a diversion. Maybe it will act like a decoy.

The antelope were still fifty yards from the water when the horse spotted them, laid its ears back, and charged, snorting and growling. The lopes almost turned inside out scattering in every direction, eyes wild, rumps flared.

I buried my head in my hands. Why me? Why a horse? Was this some divine test? I looked up as I heard the thump-clomp of hooves on the hard packed earth. My friend had returned, head high with pride for running off the smelly antelope from "our" water hole.

"Enough's, enough. At least I can tie you up to the gate a half mile down the trail."

I grabbed my sweater and jumped from the pit. The horse's eyes widened. It appeared happy to see that I was going to finally pay it some more attention. I tied the sweater around its neck and picked up my bow — the outfitter had warned me to always stay alert for rattlers on the place. A snake I could deal with. This horse thing was another matter.

We hadn't made 200 yards when the horse's ears perked and it glanced away. I peered over his back and there stood a huge buck lope; a real gagger, a hundred yards off, paying little attention to the horse with six legs. The horse veered slightly toward the buck and kept up its steady walk. I hung on to the sweater and followed, hiding behind its five-foot withers, peeking over its mane as we neared the lope. At fifty yards I snuck an arrow onto the string. The horse turned more to pass the antelope at close range. The buck paused for a moment to give the horse a curious look, then dropped its head and continued on, probably more concerned with getting a drink than an old horse it had likely seen a hundred times. Hell, they probably knew each other by name.

As if on cue the horse stopped and casually dropped its head into a clump of grass. The antelope walked past, offering a perfect 20-yard quartering away shot. The horse didn't flinch. The buck didn't jump the string. The arrow didn't miss.

Old Muddy, as I still call him today, didn't mind packing that antelope the five dusty miles back to my camp. Since that day seven years ago when the rancher sold him to me for $500, we have spent a lot of time on the bowhunting trail together.

Oh, I still hate horses. But Muddy isn't a horse, he's my hunting buddy — packs out elk, mule deer, and gets me into some of the most remote hunting spots I can find — as long as he has his favorite camo sweater around his neck. Wouldn't dream of bowhunting without him. It's just horses that I hate.

THE AMULET

Had it been any other time of day or season Sherman Dehlms probably never would have seen it. But as he sat there gazing toward the last flickers of sunset on that May evening, it shined boldly against the dull earth.

Sherman was disking the last row of his north forty and thinking more about dinner than anything else. He'd spent the afternoon on his big John Deere tractor, turning last year's chisel plowed ground into fresh turned earth ripe to accept the seed of a new soybean crop. The scent of loamy richness hung heavy in the still air as he turned and began the final pass. With less than a hundred yards to go before calling it a day, a pearly glint caught his eye.

He'd been working the ground for forty years and knew what to look for after winter's frost and spring's rains revealed treasures from the past. Even at fifty-two his eyes were still sharp enough to spot the characteristic sheen of flaked stone from atop his tractor. And this one stood out like a jewel in the evening light.

The tractor purred on idle as Sherman stepped down from the cab and walked over to the stone. Resting on a clump of soil, its worked surface reflected the low-angle beams of sunlight into a star-burst of sparkles. He plucked it from the ground and rubbed it between his fingers to remove some clinging dirt. As he held it up toward the sun, an opalescent glow filtered through the stone in changing patterns. "Damned strange one," he murmured. "Damned strange indeed."

Sherman fingered the small artifact for a moment then pocketed the find as he turned back to finish his work. Friday meant fried chicken and biscuits for dinner. His mouth was watering by the time he had disked the last hundred yards of ground into a black swath. He thought about how the freshly turned earth looked like a giant blanket of rumpled velour in the fading light. Time for home, time for chicken.

The soybeans had spread across that north forty like emerald-green waters by the time kinfolk started to arrive for the annual Fourth of July gathering on the farm. Sherman and his brother Henry were sitting in the shade of an old elm sipping iced-tea when the conversation turned to relics.

"I'll never forget the look on Dad's face when he plowed up that Mastodon tusk," Henry said. "Remember?"

"Who could forget that one. The way he came running in the house that day you would have thought he discovered a live dinosaur. Took two days to get him calmed down."

"Oh, that reminds me," Sherman continued. "I found a point this spring I want you to look at. It isn't like any of the stuff we found over the years."

He went into the house and retrieved the point from an old cigar box where he kept his hoard of artifacts. He turned it briefly in the sunlight before handing it to Henry. "With all your reading, maybe you can identify this thing. Tell me, Hank, what's the story behind it?"

Henry examined the artifact closely, grunting "I'll be darned," while he turned the small point in his hand. "This isn't just any old arrow point, Sherm. See the way its edges have been shaped. It's been worked real fine but not so it would be sharp. Made dull on purpose. The barbed end has been worked so it can hang from a thong. And this translucent stuff is nothing like the Bayport chert Indians around here used for making points. No, it isn't a regular arrow point. No sir. This thing's an amulet."

"An amu-what?"

"An amulet, Sherm. An Indian good-luck charm. They wore it around the neck. This thing probably belonged to some muckety-muck in the tribe. A big hunter or warrior. Might be worth some bucks. I still go to some of those artifact shows. Want me to see if I can get something for it?"

Sherman took back the artifact and flipped it in his hand. It wasn't doing him any good sitting in a box. Besides, with farming what it was lately, he could use a little fun money in his wallet. He held it up to the sunlight for one last look. His eyes narrowed as he gazed through the translucent point. Its milky glow changed in pattern as he tilted it back and forth, and for an instant, the image of a crouched Indian appeared...

"What's wrong, Sherm? Looks like you saw a ghost."

Sherman finally blinked, shook his head, then turned toward Henry. He quickly pocketed the point.

"Oh, it's nothing," he lied. "Just got to thinking about the years we spent bowhunting when we were young. Sometimes it seems like yesterday. Guess I'll keep this amulet thing awhile. It kind of reminds me of those days."

Sherman didn't tell a soul what he saw in the amulet that day. Hell, he wasn't even sure he'd seen anything really. Just an idle man's foolishness and aging eyes playing tricks on him.

If they were tricks, they had an odd way of reoccurring. Every evening as the sun neared the skyline, Sherman would draw the amulet from his pocket and gaze into its back-lit glow. Most of the time he saw nothing but the opaline patterns within the stone. But occasionally, when he held it just right and squinted, he saw the milky form of the crouched Indian, and sometimes he'd catch quick glimpses of the ghostly images of deer. By August the amulet had become a secret treasure Sherman feared losing, and he began wearing it on a leather thong around his neck.

One lazy Sunday while rummaging through his workshop, he came across an old recurve hidden in the rafters behind some fishing rods. He took down the bow and gently wiped off the matting of dust and spider webs. Its grip felt like the hand of an old friend.

Time hadn't harmed the Bear Kodiak. It still shined with sharp contrast between the black glass limbs and striking two-toned riser. And even after all the idle years its feel still stirred Sherman's senses. Though mice or insects had frayed the string beyond use, he pointed the bow as if aiming and went through the motions of shooting. As his fingers loosed the imaginary string, he could still see the arrow in his mind's eye leaping into space.

Sherman had long ago abandoned his passion for bowhunting when the extra work of fall's harvest began claiming all of his waking hours. As he handled the old recurve he thought back on the years. He reached up and felt the amulet through his shirt. His brow furrowed. His jaw clenched. Why should he have ever sacrificed his beloved bowhunting to spend all his time farming? The back-breaking decades of endless hours in the fields each fall hadn't made his life any better. Not by a long shot. And now as he thought about all those bowhunting seasons lost forever, he realized that if anything, his life had been less.

The next day Sherman dug through his old archery tackle and came up with a good string and a dozen Microflite arrows still sealed in the original box. He strung the bow, tested its pull. Godalmighty, it felt good. Sure, he'd put on some girth over the years but his farm-hewn shoulders and arms still responded easily to the pull of the bow. Like riding bikes and milking cows, some things in life stay with a man forever.

He set up some bales behind the barn and attached a paper plate to the center. He stepped back twenty paces, nocked an arrow, and drew. Sherman aimed with rock-steady arms for close to a minute before letting the string down and replacing the arrow in his hip pocket. He hadn't forgotten how to shoot the bow. A paper plate on the bales just didn't seem like the proper thing to shoot at. For no particular reason he turned and headed for a nearby stubble field. There he drew. There he shot. And aiming at clumps of grass, he did both like never before.

Sherman knew he had never shown classic shooting form, and he simply passed off his strange new technique as a result of aging. A man my age skiing or bicycling, he thought, would likely hug the ground more than a youngster. Guess the same thing holds true for archery. With that he leaned into the draw of another arrow, hunched over in his new shooting form, its draw pitifully short. Nonetheless, his arrow again sailed to the mark with uncanny grace.

With his reborn passion, late summer swept by quickly for Sherman. By September his thoughts naturally turned to the approaching harvest. Appeared to be a banner year for corn. Beans looked like bushel-breakers too. But Sherman also began pondering another harvest as old as mankind — that of the deer. Friends thought he had slipped prematurely into his second childhood when he purchased a bowhunting license and made a dozen wooden hunting arrows. The week before season opened he spent his evenings practicing in the stubble field, resharpening his broadheads, and peering through the amulet at sunset.

The occasional image of the Indian shooting in the hunched over pose grew fainter as autumn's sun swung more northerly in the sky. But with its faded image, the wavering images of deer drifted within the reflections of the amulet almost every evening. And with each journey into the amulet's glow, Sherman gained a thirst for the hunt beyond any he had known as a young man.

Opening morning found him easing toward a blind he had built weeks before. He was too old to be dangling from trees like some kid. As he neared the blind, the grayness of morning began melting into daybreak, revealing a hazy fog that hugged the ground. Sherman passed the blind without a glance. He drifted among the shadows, eased between the trees like the ebbing fog. He couldn't remember sneaking along with such grace as a younger man. Maybe the years had made him wise to the virtues of patience and timing. His eyes dissected every patch of brush as he moved. He spotted crouched rabbits, hiding pheasants, and more game than he had ever seen in the woods. Though years on roaring tractors had dulled his hearing, his ears filtered out the subtle sounds of dew drops, falling leaves, woodpeckers — and approaching hooves.

Sherman melted into the shadows of a wild grape cluster as three whitetails appeared in a small clearing. He felt the coolness of the amulet against his breastbone. He nocked an arrow. He squinted his eyes. He pressed his lips. And much to his surprise, he gave the gentle call of a fawn.

With no time for thought he let a flood of reactions wash over him. A doe approached, head canted in curiosity. When she passed behind a thornapple tree, Sherman drew. The deer stepped clear. The arrow leaped to its mark. Moments later, Sherman's mouth began to water. He thought that odd. It wasn't fried-chicken Friday and dinner was a long way off. He rolled up his sleeves, and began taking care of his early harvest.

In the weeks that followed, Sherman enjoyed a bumper harvest from the fields too. Drying beans and plowing under corn stubble kept him busy and fall passed quicker than ever. Thanksgiving came before he knew it. Kinfolk again gathered at the farm.

"What's this I hear we're having venison with our turkey this year?" Henry said. "Word's out you're going off the deep end, Sherm, acting like some kid or savage with all this bowhunting stuff."

Sherman just grinned with a smile that reflected the wisdom of ages. "Don't worry, Hank. I haven't gone off the deep end. If anything I avoided it. I also rediscovered a piece of myself that's been there all along."

"Well, whatever it is, you're looking better than I've seen you in years. Must be the banner harvest you had this year took some weight off your mind."

"It sure did," Sherman said, lifting his nose to the aroma of roast venison. "It's been one dandy of a sweet harvest this season. I've never seen or felt one like it. It's like the ones we knew as kids, only richer because I'm old enough to appreciate it more."

With a far away look in his eye the conversation drifted to other topics. By the time they were sipping coffee after dinner, talk drifted to relics.

"Changed your mind about trying to sell that amulet, Sherm?"

"Couldn't change it if I wanted. I don't have it anymore. Gave it to some guy I let bowhunt in the woodlot near the north forty. With the way he was stumbling around the woods I figured he needed a little help finding out what bowhunting was really all about."

Henry cocked his head and crumpled his brow. "And you think that somehow giving him that thing is going help?"

"Got a strong hunch it just might. A real strong hunch."

"Well, isn't that something? You give away a valued artifact to some guy you hardly know. How do you know he won't sell it?"

"The deal was he could keep it until he took a deer then he had to pass it on to another bowhunter. After my harvest this season I realized that the amulet wasn't meant to be owned, just used to free the real bowhunter lurking within all of us, then passed along. No, he won't sell it."

Sherman Dehlms turned and gazed out the window. He didn't notice his brother giving him an odd stare. Wouldn't care if he did. The sun was just touching the leaf-bare tree line. He squinted, the bronze rays blurring in his vision. And for an instant, the image of an Indian stood on the horizon, smiling. Sherman smiled back.

Near the north forty, a young bowhunter crouched and drew. The coolness of the amulet pressed against his breastbone. Even before releasing his arrow into the fading shadows, his mouth began to water.

THE PROMISE

As Pete brushed the snow from his arrow, he realized he had never loved or hated the woods more. He wished he could be anyplace else, yet knew there was no other place he could be. He'd promised he would hunt. So he stared blankly into the swirling snow, his thoughts drifting back to last spring.

"Hey, Petey," Dave had said during their spring scouting. "Check out this magnum rub."

Dave had stood grinning next to a five-inch cedar stripped bare to the sapwood. "Looks like The Rake made a rub line along this thicket last fall. See how his burr tines have gouged this cedar. I bet other bucks tuck their tails when they see this dude coming."

Raising his eyebrows, Pete smiled at Dave before running his fingers over the scarred tree. Sure enough, the deep marks low on the trunk looked like the work of The Rake. They had spotted the deer one evening the year before while driving back to the cabin. It stood frozen in the glow of headlights, its massive rack sporting clusters of gnarled burr tines and rows of closely packed points, looking more like a giant garden rake than antlers. It etched a vivid portrait in the two bowhunter's minds before loping into the darkness.

Pete had peered deeper into the tangle of Lostlogger Swamp. "Look, more rubs along that alder patch. They weren't there in November when I hunted near the creek. You s'pose he ruts late here?"

Dave looked over Pete's shoulder. "Probably makes his rounds through the swamp during mid-December looking for doe-fawns in their first heat. The guy's a real cradle robber."

They snickered.

"Then he probably made it through gun season and might be back in the fall."

"More like next December," Dave said. "He ruts later than most bucks. We can catch him here after the snow drives him from those aspen hills. He's made it through lots of gun seasons. He'll be back. I'd bet a dozen cedar arrows on it."

During their scouting trips, Dave always found the best spots. He always found the biggest sheds too. But Pete didn't mind. Not one bit, because Dave's discoveries were always partly his. They shared everything: campfires, rub lines, sheds, scrapes, bowhunting gear — all the good stuff in life. They had since the day they left their mother's womb just minutes apart: identical twins, magically bonded. They could read each other's thoughts, feel each other's joys, excitement and sorrows.

It was after that spring scouting trip that Dave returned home unusually tired. Pete noticed first. His brother looked pale, especially for a rugged 20-year-old who was always blazing a trail through life. For him the promise of another spring didn't bloom. Dave was diagnosed with leukemia.

Summer swept by like an ashen dream: new doctors, more tests, barely a thread of hope — stuff that was only supposed to happen to someone else, people in movies, not his brother. Then the thread of hope snapped, an unsuccessful transplant of Pete's marrow. And Pete couldn't shake the guilt; he had failed Dave miserably.

With hope all but gone, Dave faded like fall's colors. By mid-December he appeared a thin reflection of his brother. Pete hovered near Dave's bedside like a shadow until Dave begged him to leave.

"Come on, Petey, please. Please do it for me. We spent way too much time patterning The Rake to let him slip away now. The way it's snowing outside he's gotta be in Lostlogger Swamp. Dad already said he'd go to the cabin with you."

Shaking his head, Pete struggled with the words, "I can't. Not without you. What if while I'm gone you..."

Dave cut him off, a touch of anger in his voice. "Look, I'm not asking you to have fun. Just go sit in the stand. It's my only chance to feel the thrill of bowhunting again — through you. Wherever you go, part of me goes. It's always been that way, always will be. For us, Petey. Go get The Rake. Say you will. Promise."

Pete saw a shine in Dave's eyes he hadn't seen for months. "Okay, I'll go," he finally said, his words crackling at first, gaining resolve as he grabbed his jacket. "I'll go for us. And you get ready to feast on Rake steaks when I get back. And THAT'S a promise."

He had left Dave with the fire in his eyes still burning brightly.

Now, 200 miles later in the frozen recesses of Lostlogger Swamp, Pete looked down from his jack pine stand. Dave had been right about the buck. Fresh rubs marked The Rake's old travel lane. Dave had also been right about sharing in the hunt. Pete looked at the quiver full of cedar arrows they had made together. "You are here aren't you, Dave?" he whispered. He gripped the recurve they shared and clenched his jaw. "Maybe, Dave, maybe we can fill the promise together."

The snow turned into stinging needles of ice as the final hour of daylight faded into grayness. Pete was gazing at the simple lines of his two-blade broadhead when he noticed a distant shadow drifting in the cedars. At first he thought it was another snow swirl. But there it was again, closer, grayer than the icy backdrop. Suddenly the realization struck him —The Rake.

Pete barely had time to shake himself free of the cold before The Rake sauntered into the shooting lane. As Pete drew, everything clicked into slow-motion. Ice crystals drifted lazily past his face. The Rake floated into the opening like a gray cloud. Pete's fingers slipped from the string. The arrow leaped, feathers pinwheeling through the cold air. The dull thump of broadhead biting buckskin snapped Pete's senses back.

The buck flinched and spun hard, snow spraying in its path. In a flash The Rake was gone. The tangle of cedars swallowed it with barely a sound. Only the whisper of a raw wind filled the evening.

By the time Pete gathered his gear and took up the trail, darkness and a bitter cold had settled over the swamp. With his flashlight beam knifing the night, Pete plowed through the knee-deep snow, following crimson specks. A hundred yards into the swamp, The Rake burst from under a deadfall and bolted across a creek. Pete fumbled for an arrow. The buck melted into the night before he could nock it. Damn, I've got a promise to keep. How can that buck be so tough a survivor when my brother lies there dying? It doesn't make sense. Pete pushed deeper into the swamp.

He jumped the buck twice more before it crossed the creek again, still eluding another arrow. Come on, die you old buck, your time's up. Let me keep this promise. Pete pressed on. So dark, so far, maybe I should give up the trail until morning, get Dad's help. I suppose that's what Dave would do. But no, it's my promise to keep, not Dad's. Besides, Dave's with me and the buck's slowing, it can't last much longer. Pete headed for the creek.

He leaped for a log near the far bank, but his foot slipped, throwing him sideways into the water. With soaked forearms and legs, Pete clambered up the bank, cursing the cold. Dumb trick. He could almost hear Dave laughing. Pete shook his head. He wrung out his gloves and continued on.

A hundred yards from the creek, he spotted The Rake laying near a fallen cedar. Pete nocked an arrow. He stood watching the great buck for a long time but it didn't stir, didn't breathe. He inched closer. The first arrow had hit tight behind the shoulder, a fatal wound. How had The Rake made it so far? Why did it last so long? He reached out and stroked the buck's massive neck — a true survivor to the end. Finally, The Rake was his, their's. He'd kept the promise.

The hot insides of the buck stung Pete's numbed hands. He let out a long groan then looked skyward. The clouds had cleared. Stars twinkled overhead.

"This one's for you, Dave," he whispered, his breath gathering in a steamy cloud. The temperature was dropping fast.

By the time Pete finished dressing the deer, the crusted snow on his damp jacket and pants had frozen. He tried pulling on his gloves and found them stiff. He jammed his hands inside them anyway and began dragging the buck toward an old logging trail — a shortcut he thought would save time. But after an hour of stumbling through the snowy swamp he came to another creek. This looks too deep. I can't remember seeing it before. Now what? I'm not about to get wet again.

He began backtracking his swath in the snow. Even though it was easier dragging the huge buck on broken trail, cold and exhaustion soon took their toll. Pete's damp arms and legs grew prickly numb. His breath came in heaving gasps as he began floundering with the buck. And finally, after each step became a painful struggle, Pete abandoned the buck and plodded on.

Later, he stopped to rub his hands together. The bow! Where's our bow? You idiot, you lost it. What's wrong with you? Find it, quick. What did you do with it? He charged frantically back on his tracks, lurching through the snow. Panting and cursing, he found the bow only a short ways from the buck. Admit it, you're lost too. He looked down at his frozen arms and legs. You'll never make it 'til morning now. You blew it. You're finished. He crawled over and sat on the now-frozen whitetail and began to sob. I'm sorry, Dave, so sorry. He curled up. Moments later a great sleep overtook him.

"Hey, Petey," a voice echoed in his ears. "Get your butt moving before you become another legend of Lostlogger Swamp. You and The Rake deserve a better end than this!"

Pete cracked an eyelid and peered into the darkness. Only ghostly shapes of snow-draped cedars surrounded him. "Who's there?" he mumbled, his voice hoarse and weak.

"Don't gimme that old 'I'm sleepy routine,'" rang Dave's voice. "It's time to celebrate our harvesting of The Rake."

Pete propped himself up on an elbow and tried clicking on his flashlight. No use. The cold had sapped its life. He unfolded his stiff body and stood. His senses felt dull and achy. "Where are you, Dave?"

"Over here behind the wall of cedars. I've found a great place to camp. Come on in and start a fire."

Pete stumbled toward Dave's voice. Plowing through the matting of cedars he discovered a giant pile of deadfalls crisscrossed together.

"In here Petey, it's open under here like the brush forts we built when we were kids, remember?"

Pete stooped and entered an opening in the tangled mass of trees. Inside it was black but he wasn't afraid. Dave was there somewhere.

"Where are you Dave, how'd you get here?" Pete's words came in an incoherent slur yet they were answered.

"I'm right next to you, silly. Now get a fire going. It's colder than a chic-a-dee's butt in February in here."

Pete struggled to clear his mind. "Can't make fire. My only matches won't light. Already tried earlier, no use. Too damp. Too cold."

"Then it's a dang good thing you're wearing my lucky jacket," said Dave. "You never could keep from grabbing the wrong one. Just reach inside the rear zipper pouch, there's a disposable lighter and a fire starter stick in there. These dry birch and cedar branches in here ought to burn like blazes."

With nearly frozen hands, Pete fumbled in the darkness for minutes before finally flicking the lighter to life and lighting the fire starter. He added handfuls of cedar twigs that quickly crackled into bright flames. The fire's glow filled the small fortress. In one corner sat a snowshoe hare, a few weeks short of reaching its full all white phase, its eyes reflecting back the fire's light. In the other corner sat Dave.

"Pretty neat in here, hey Petey?"

Pete squinted into the smoke and shook his head. His mind ached with a dull buzz. There on a log sat Dave, the same Dave that Pete had known last spring. He appeared full of life and vigor. Pete sank to his knees and held his hands over the fire. As he wiggled warmth back into his fingers, Dave leaned close to the fire, the smile on his face brighter than ever.

"Great shot, Petey, but you trailed him too soon. You should have waited until morning and let Dad help. He'll be pissed that you got lost and spent the night out."

"How did you know I was lost? How did you know I got The Rake?" Pete reached up and tried rubbing the numbness from his temples.

"Remember, Petey? Wherever you go, I go. Whatever you do, I do. That's what will always be special about us. I'm part you, you're part me. We're one heck of a bowhunting team; always will be. Now what do you say we get down to some real celebrating. Go strip out those buck fillets and let's have some campfire venison like the old days."

In a blur of exhaustion and cold, Pete sat with Dave near the fire. Long into the night they ate roast deer meat and talked over the fire's glow, its warmth filling the snow-blanketed shelter. They sang campfire songs and reminisced about hunts past, planned hunts anew. Sometime in the night a great sleep overcame them.

Pete woke to the cold dripping of melting snow on his forehead and a voice outside. Slivers of light poked through several small openings in the deadfall maze. He turned and looked around, but Dave wasn't there. Maybe that's him outside?

He stumbled outside and squinted against a brilliant sun. His Dad's frantic voice cut through the still air.

"I'm over here, Dad. Over here!"

His Dad burst through the wall of cedars, eyes ringed and red, his face haggard. "For the love of God, Pete, I thought we lost you too."

"I'm okay, Dad. We spent the night just fine. Me and Dave even had roast —"

Pete stopped short at the pain in his Dad's eyes.

"I'm sorry son, Dave's gone. I got word from the sheriff last night after dark. I drove to town and was on the phone with your mother half the night. Spent the other half looking for you. The wind and snow covered most of your tracks. It was a good thing I found that orange flagging you left marking your way into the swamp."

"But I didn't —"

Pete reached deep into one of his jacket pockets, Dave's pocket he realized, and pulled out a roll of fluorescent surveyor's ribbon he didn't know was there. Half of it was used.

He put his arms around his dad and they quietly held each other for a long time.

Then the three of them dragged The Rake from Lostlogger Swamp.

WHITETAIL UTOPIA

Utopia is supposed to be an imaginary place of perfection, merely wishful thinking. Yet somehow there it laid before me in three-dimensional splendor — the perfect whitetail spot.

I'd searched for such a place for years. Driven by the writings of whitetail masters, I'd scoured half the woodlots in Southern Michigan, only finding a handful of good spots. Nothing came close to the utopia I discovered in a small clearing that November afternoon. A maze of track-churned trails spoked into the clearing from every direction, terminating in a giant scrape under a lone thornapple tree. Though I'd never seen one before, there was no mistaking it. I'd discovered the mother lode, the end of the rainbow, a whitetailer's gold mine in the leaves. I'd found a hub scrape.

My mind reeled as I tried grasping the magnificence of the thing. The place looked and smelled like a barnyard for bucks. Every sapling within twenty yards wore the fresh wounds of rut-crazed bruisers, and the overhanging branches on the thornapple hung twisted and limp. Some still shined from deer spit. And to top off the entire scene, a God-sent elm stood twenty yards downwind of the havoc, its heavy branches forking fifteen feet up — the perfect setup over the perfect place. Double utopia. A bowhunter's dream.

A flagpole-sized sapling grew along side the stately elm, offering an ideal shinnying pole to the forked crotch. No need for tree steps. The rough bark on the sapling offered sure-grip handholds. I donned rubber gloves and easily shinnied up to the elm's fork, quickly setting my portable stand. Everything looked perfect.

I found the place none too soon. The rut was approaching its peak and a cold front was forecast to move through during the night. The perfect weather, at the perfect spot, at the perfect time. Tomorrow morning promised triple utopia. As I snuck away into the afternoon shadows, I knew whitetail greatness awaited me.

That night, as I dreamed of giant bucks and short blood trails, a sticky snow swirled across the countryside, spraying the landscape with a white frosting that stuck to everything before freezing into a crystalline mass. I woke to a whitetailer's wonderland.

An hour before daylight, I crunched my way under ghostly drooping branches. Great white arms of oaks and maples gestured to pat me on the back, already congratulating me on the huge buck I was about to claim. The crisp air that morning even held a eerie thread of tension, foretelling of unforgettable events about to unfold.

Near the clearing, I hardly recognized the big elm holding my stand. Its snow-clad branches hung like the weary arms of a fighter in the tenth round. I shined a flashlight beam on the scrape. It looked untouched. Perfect, at first light he'll be mine.

I set down my bow, pack, and portable tree seat, and tied them to my pull-up rope. Putting on my rubber gloves, I stepped back a few paces, and leaped up the sapling. For a split second I felt the excitement of soaring upward. A second later, I slid back down. I hit the ground with a "thump" and looked up just in time to catch a face full of snow dumping from the branches. I gasped at the sting as I dug at the snow inching down my collar. The sapling glistened with ice.

I leaped again, higher this time, only to slide down twice as fast. I felt a hot flush rising in my cheeks. Okay, fun's over. Now I'm getting mad. Off came the gloves. Furious, I jumped up the sapling again and again, digging my fingers into the frozen bark until my fingertips turned blue with pain. It was no use. The sapling, cold and indifferent to my rage, just stood there swaying back and forth, its icy sheath glimmering brighter than ever.

Sweat tricked down my forehead. Then it dawned on me. My clothes! My bulky clothes must be holding me back. To ward off the frigid weather I was dressed like the Pillsbury Dough Boy with so many layers I could barely move, let alone climb. So I stripped off my jacket, vest, and sweater, and lashed them to my pack.

A wave of frigid air swept through my damp shirt, chilling me into a sense of exhilaration. No sense crying about tree steps that were an hour round-trip away and sitting back home. Time to use some determination instead. I rubbed my numbed hands until my fingertips burned. Okay, let's get the lead out, whitetailer. You're scenting up utopia. Now get your butt skyward.

Again I leaped up the tree. This time I dug my fingernails in for all I was worth and madly pulled myself up. Several feet below the stand, my arms knotted and the feeling began draining from my fingers. I gritted my teeth, grunted, and with one final pull, made it to the stand.

Steadying myself against the trunk, I tied my safety rope around the elm, further numbing my hands with more fresh snow. I almost laughed at the pain — ha, I'd won the battle. With little feeling left, I pulled up the heavy bundle of bow, pack, clothes, and portable seat.

Working against the cold with fingers like hibernating spiders, I untied my Bear recurve and hung it on a limb. I then untied my pack with its glob of clothing and innocently set it on the edge of the stand. While the last bit of feeling faded from my hands, I untied the portable seat and started lashing it to the tree.

Then it happened.

With numbed reflexes, I watched unbelieving as the seat slipped from my grip, whacking the stand loudly before fiendishly catching my pack and clothes, tumbling the whole mess into the snow below. Suddenly my dream hunt began mutating into a nightmare. The sun began rising. Utopia was fading fast.

Enraged at the ice, cold, and my carelessness, I untied my safety rope, grabbed the sapling, and stepped off the stand. Another mistake. I plummeted to the ground faster than a fat kid on a greased flag pole.

Kerthump!

I sprawled into the snow, making an abstract snow angel with broken wings. As I rolled slowly over, trying to regain my wind, the whole thing suddenly seemed cute, even funny. The deformed snow angel, the iced sapling, the white trees all staring at the floundering bowhunter — some utopia, what a joke. Lapsing into laughter, I failed to recognize the first stage of hypothermia.

Still snickering, I again tied my seat and pack to my pull-up rope and leaped for the sapling. I knew I wouldn't make it. It was slicker than ever. No sense freezing to death, so I untied my seat and pack and put my clothes back on. I regained some of my senses and began hopping around, flailing my arms, trying to get my molasses-thick blood flowing. Soon, it began to work. My mind started clicking.

Okay, snow-squirrel, no sense trying to climb up to the tree stand. I'll just have to find some promising log to hunt behind. Besides, this spot is so fantastic it probably doesn't matter where I sit. But as I turned to leave, a new rush of blood finally cleared my brain — my bow! Where's my bow? I spun around looking in the snow. Then, I groaned as I looked up. There it was, still hanging in the tree. Utopia never dangled so hauntingly.

At that moment I would have given my lucky camo hat for my tree steps or even a chain saw. I even toyed with the idea of using my small pruning saw on the big elm. Naw. That would take all morning and would probably end up breaking my bow or worse yet felling the tree on myself. Forget it. It's about as dumb as using your knife. What? Yeah, my knife!

I pulled my knife from my pack and began chopping off the layer of crusted ice from the sapling. Foot by foot, I shinnied up the sapling, hacking away as I went. After a half-hour of struggling, I climbed wobbly-legged into my tree stand. Success! And just in time too. The sun's pale rays began filtering through the white lace-work of branches.

Still panting, I lashed myself to the big elm and paused long enough to mentally kick myself in the butt for missing first shooting light. But maybe the buck would come by yet. Sure, this snow has probably slowed him down and he'll be strolling by any time now. All I need to do is get these frozen hands working and I'll be able to arrow him.

Sparked with a new glimmer of hope, I reached down and yanked on my pull-up rope. A new wave of nausea flooded over me. The rope felt pitifully light. The end dangled freely. There, on the ground, five feet from the tree, lay my tree seat and opened pack, complete with heavy gloves, shooting glove, hand warmer, thermos of cocoa, and snacks. I whimpered at the sight.

Weary, light-headed, and drained of my last drop of hope, I wanted to leap into the snowy web-work and end the pain. But I just stood staring at all those unused runways leading to the scrape blanketed under the untracked snow. As I gazed below, a fleeting thought surfaced. The rope! My bow! Maybe I could hook my pack with it and still save the day before Mr. Big sauntered by?

I tied the rope around my bowstring near the upper tip and lowered the bow. I began swinging it back and forth, getting nearer to the pack with each swing. On the final outward arc, I dropped the bow on the pack. Perhaps I could catch one of the straps or maybe the buckle between the limb and bowstring? What I caught instead was the tip of my pruning saw sticking out from the pack — my new saw with the laser-sharpened teeth. I barely tugged on it when the string exploded in a hissing snap, springing the bow off the rope and into the snow.

Just as I was about to scream, a flicker of brown in the glazed branches stopped me cold. A line of does nervously filtered between the frosted thornapples and passed on the far side of the scrape. Only a button buck bringing up the rear ventured into the scrape and pawed for a second before skittering after the herd.

Moments later, dark legs threaded between snowy trunks. Nose to the ground and eyes glazed with love, a rangy 10-pointer ambled out of the whiteness.

He looked "book" all the way. After bullying a nearby sapling, he strutted toward my pack and bow, head canted in curiosity. He visibly stiffened as he neared the pack. Spotting my angel pattern in the snow, he jerked his head back and forth, staring at the angel print, my pack, then back to my bow. Finally, as if a light bulb clicked on behind that furry forehead, he snapped up his head and looked right through me.

He had me. I gave in to the futility of it all.

"Hell of a mornin', ain't it?" I said.

He whirled, and in two great bounds, disappeared into the whiteness.

As I slid/fell down the sapling for the final time and gathered up my gear, sunbeams lanced through holes in the white maze. Instantly, the entire forest came alive in a million karats of nature's twinkling gem-work. I knew more than ever that utopia was only supposed to be an imaginary placc of perfection. Yet somehow I also knew I was witnessing a rare piece of it. It may not have been whitetail utopia, but at that moment it was utopia just the same.

CHARLIE'S CAP

Charlie turned toward the sound. It barely rustled the leaves, like spider legs softly creeping. He strained to listen. It grew louder as if a breeze were ebbing then rushing anew, stirring ever closer. He swallowed. It couldn't be a breeze. Evening's calm had claimed the forest for almost an hour, a deathly calm that for some reason had even hushed the twilight calls of chick-a-dees. It drew closer. With only fifteen minutes of shooting light left, it must be deer.

He reached to grab his bow hanging on the stub of a branch. Well, it wasn't his bow really. He had borrowed the thing from his cousin along with a half-dozen arrows. Nonetheless, it officially made him a bowhunter now, the big rage among the guys at the shop these days. Charlie tightened his fingers on the string. Closer now, the rustling grew, the faint steps of feet crunching through October's leaves.

Charlie looked down from his stand in the big oak. The chewed acorns laying among the rumpled leaves must have been the work of deer. He shook his head. Why did the guys at the shop make such a big deal out of bowhunting deer? Like it was some great mystery finding the perfect ambush then arrowing one of the things? Some mystery. What a bunch of nerds. All they had to do was look at the sign, for cripes sake. In a few seconds I'll show them there's no mystery to it at all. The footsteps shuffled closer, only yards away. A shadow materialized from the underbrush. Charlie raised the bow.

He cussed under his breath when a raccoon stepped clear of the brush. Damned coon. The thing had set off all the deer alarms in his head, making his heart race and palms sweat.

More rustling. He raised the bow again. Alright, maybe the final minutes of light would produce a deer after all. Damn it again. Charlie sighed as another coon scurried from the brush and joined the first, snarling and clawing for some tidbit probably. Then three more emerged and neared the rest, their little hands searching under the leaves.

Five in all, must be a family. But now with a full summer's growth on their bones and all that fat rounding them out, I can't tell the difference between the yearlings and their mother — not that it matters now. The damned things made me feel like an idiot and primed my pump to shoot. And even without a small game license, by God an arrow I'm going to shoot.

With the anti-fur movement the past few years, coon pelts weren't worth a can of beans and the pests had flourished like rabbits. Now five of the buggers. Too bad I don't have an extra quiver full of arrows to waste on the varmints. I'd bloody the woods proper with them. He looked at the four broadheads in his quiver. Okay, one will do. These arrows cost too much to waste on coons. Hell, you can't even eat the greasy things. The only thing they're good for is making coonskin caps.

Charlie suddenly pictured himself wearing a great pile of coon fur atop his head, strutting into the shop and showing the guys what kind of bowhunter he was. Yeah, a coonskin cap, that'll make them take notice, big time. Sure, I'll show them who's a bowhunter.

For a moment Charlie looked for the biggest. What the hell, size doesn't matter that much. Any of them will make a fine cap. Better to shoot the closest. Can't afford a miss, not if I want that reputation of being a killer-diller. He drew and tried to steady his aim. Damned things kept moving so much it was like trying to aim at butterflies flitting in the wind. They snarled and nipped at one another, twisted and squirmed. Vicious little buggers. Anything that mean deserves some cold steel. He shot.

An enraged snarl much too loud for the small thing filled the evening as the arrow bit too far back, pinning the coon to the ground. Holy crap, listen to that thing. Geez, it's loud. The raccoon twisted and bit savagely at the arrow holding it, foamy spittle flying wildly from its jaws as the sharp teeth snapped the shaft in half. Before it could wiggle free, the other coons seized upon it, suddenly becoming a frenzied bundle of fur, teeth and claws tearing the life from the arrowed coon. Seconds later it lay a tattered mess of a thing, its fur and insides mixed together like jumbled pieces of a jigsaw puzzle. A ruined arrow. A ruined cap. Crazy-assed things. Why would they do that?

Charlie watched in confusion as the four remaining coons turned on one another now, bristled and biting like enraged dogs. In the poor light, he failed to notice the foamed spittle in their mouths, the insane fury in their little eyes. With all this commotion, the coons would spoil this spot for good. I can't have that. I'll show you little bastards. He shot again.

His arrow missed but the sharp twang of his bowstring splitting the calm air stopped the coon's fighting. In unison, they arched their backs like spooked alley cats, tails puffed, hair standing on end. They stood rooted for a moment, their beady eyes searching up in the branches for the sound.

"Go on, beat it, assholes! You're spoiling my hunt." Charlie waved his arms and twisted his face at the coons.

One by one, they locked onto his form in the tree. Then one after another, they charged up the oak after him.

Quicker than young bears, they surged up the tree, claws ripping bark as they came. What the hell? Charlie stood dumbfounded for a moment, then realized what he should have all along. Crap, rabid coons, get away, get away. He fumbled to nock another arrow on the string. He cussed as he dropped it. Now I remember, recent outbreaks of rabies — another good reason to kill the things. He grabbed for another arrow as the first coon came over the edge of his tree stand and seized his leg. Ouch, damn it. Instinctively, he kicked and tried to rid his leg of the thing. But it clung with a savage fury as the fangs chewed deep into his calf. His scream echoed through the woods.

In one swift motion, Charlie raised his leg and swung the bow down with all his might. The two remaining arrows flew from the bowquiver as the limb struck the coon solidly. It let out a half whimper, half snarl as its grip faltered and it fell to the ground, dazed. Charlie spun to the sound of bark shredding near his ear as another coon rushed around the tree and jumped on his back. He swatted at the thing as he felt teeth bite deep into his shoulder. He hollered and staggered backward in panic. He fell.

The safety belt ripped at his waist as he hit the end of the three-foot tether. It jerked the wind from him. His head buzzed. He sucked for air. By the time he regained his senses, the coons were around him again, reaching from the branches, biting and clawing as he floundered upside down in the safety belt. Charlie swatted the things at bay as if he were being ravaged by a hive of killer bees. In final desperation, he clawed at the release of his safety belt. Free at last, he floated away from the attacking coons. So long, assholes.

He swung his arms wildly trying to right himself to land on his feet instead of his head. Good, you're going to make it.

CRACK! A large oak limb near the ground interrupted his fall. The sharp impact stunned his lower back. Man, that didn't hurt half as bad as it sounded. He tumbled over the branch in slow motion. He heard the snap and wondered why the branch was still there, not even cracked. He hit the ground face down, the musky aroma of the forest floor filling his head.

He laid there for a moment, panting, regaining his breath. There, that wasn't such a bad fall. The scratching of claws descending the tree reached his ears. Crap, here they come again. Not this time you little bastards. He began scrambling to his feet. He struggled to draw his legs up under him and push up on his arms. Come on, man, hurry up, run, get going, What the hell's wrong? Crap, my back!

Charlie's mind was running for his life, yet his body just laid there, a numb wad of flesh, hearing, seeing, knowing what he should do but unable to do it.

The coons seemed to sense his plight. They didn't attack with the frenzy they had shown in the tree. Now they went about their task almost business-like. Nearby, the dazed coon staggered to its feet. The thing waddled over to Charlie's face and looked into his eyes, only inches away. Go on, get back, or I'll bite your ass. Charlie struggled to bare his teeth. His tongue barely moved. The depths of the coon's eyes held a hatred that made the hair rise along Charlie's neck. The little eyes probed his for a moment before the thing snarled and joined the others out of Charlie's line of sight. Their shadows on the leaves looked like elongated figures of elves busy at work. Hey, get off. What are you doing back there? Stop it.

They snarled. Clothes ripped. Flesh began to tear, but he felt nothing wrong. Teeth crunched something. Once through the layer of clothes, the coons ate faster. Driven by instinct and the early stages of insanity, their mouths made anxious smacking sounds as they greedily consumed the offering before them. So much fat to build before winter's grip set in and now so much protein wonderfully laid before them.

Hey, I'm the hunter here, not you assholes. Now beat it before I get that bow and gut-shoot all of you. Charlie worked his mouth but the words barely trickled out in a low hiss. Hat hell, I'll kill the whole bunch of you and make a coat. The guys at the shop will really take notice then. Yeah, a raccoon coat, that's what I'll do to you, all of you. He laid there gasping for air, letting the rage fill his mind completely.

The coons moved off to the side, tugging and snarling over some morsel. What? Listen, they're leaving. Something crunching. Yes, take it and leave you little bastards. Wait until I get better. Just wait until I come back to settle the score. This ain't over. I'll bloody the woods with you, all of your kind.

The coons waddled back into his line of sight. Charlie gasped. How did they get that? Hey, asshole, that's mine. You can't have that.

Rage clouded his mind. He watched unblinking as the coons chewed the fingers of his detached hand, nibbling his digits like spareribs.

Suddenly a tingle of feeling rippled down his back. What? Yes, I can feel my legs. Now you little son-of-a-bitches are going to pay big time. I'm going to kick your asses into next week!

Charlie's feet twitched. He turned his head. Payback time, assholes. The coons stopped munching at the movement. They dropped the remains of his hand, stood on their haunches like miniature grizzlies ready to reclaim their prize. Charlie drew a leg under him. One more, that's it. Now I'll show them, oversized rats.

The coons dropped to all fours and charged. They swarmed upon the sweetness of Charlie's head and face. His feet twitched for only a moment as he went down for the last time.

For a while he wore a grand coonskin cap. When they had picked the skull clean, they moved to his torso like a great coat, eating as they went.

Surprisingly, Charlie had worn both cap and coat from the same coons — a remarkable feat for a first-time bowhunter.

GREENER PASTURES

There weren't many bowhunters greener to south Texas than me and my javelina sidekick, Toad. It was our first trip there.

Toad's real name is Dave or Fred, maybe even Sam. Don't know for sure and it really doesn't matter. He's been Toad forever and probably always will be. He got the name as a kid because of his enormous wide set green eyes and the oversized mouth that stretched from one side of his face to the other. It hung in a perpetual gape, spittle collecting at the corners as if he were always ready to snatch some passing bug. Even his squat form and bow-legged gait add to the image. Where childhood looks spawned Toad's nickname, becoming an adult cemented it. Age enhanced his toady features. He even sported three oversized moles on his brow that looked just like genuine toad warts. But despite his amphibian looks, Toad was the best bowhunting buddy a guy could hope for. He'd follow you to the meanest place on earth for the chance to arrow a snake or roadrunner — anything that ate toads, Toad hated.

And now, that mean place bounced in the headlights of the truck as our south Texas guide, Joe, drove further into the cactus.

"Now don't you boys get to thinkin' them pastures are greener on the other side of that west fence," Joe said, a slight dribble of morning chew sputtering past his lips. "This here cactus patch I'm takin' ya to holds plenty of adventure for a couple of northern slicks like y'awl."

He wiped his chin with a gloved hand and peered back over the steering wheel into the predawn gloom. For a javelina guide, Joe had it all; words that rolled like tumble weeds, the charm of a barbed wire fence, and a face like the cactus dancing in the headlights. Prickly whiskers covered his puffed cheeks, narrow slits sat where most men wore eyes. A sweat-stained Stetson shadowed his oversized ears and bristly gray hair. Even the faded bandana bunched around his neck looked like part of the arid brush country churning under the tires. But the real clue to Joe's life were the deeply etched wrinkles rimming his eyes and mouth. They spoke of his 40 years of punching longhorns in the Texas sun, spittin' tobacco, and moving herds to greener pastures. He'd spent most his life on old-time cattle drives. But progress, fences, and cold-storage trucks ended all that. Now he passed his days raising a few prized longhorns and guiding greenhorn bowhunters to help make ends meet.

Lit by the first trickles of light from the east, a vast expanse of cactus and twisted mesquite lay before us in the sprawling brush country that had once been the stomping ground of desert Indians; Santa Anna, and Pancho Villa. Before day's end we too would join that legendary roster of men who had faced the perils of this harsh land, leaving behind their mark in time. We'd come a long way to arrow a javelina. By sunset this strange land would be part of us, we part of it.

Joe turned off the engine and coasted his old pickup to a halt. He flicked off the headlights. We sat in silence. The clumps of prickly pear took on the gray shapes of weird creatures and the mesquite waved skeleton arms in the morning breeze.

"Okay, slicks," Joe finally said, "time for y'awl to get your sleepy backsides movin' through that cactus. Them pigs ain't had breakfast yet and I reckon a couple of dudes like y'awl might taste pretty damned good to 'em."

Joe spat out the window and cackled at his wit. Toad and I gave him a sideways scowl.

"Now you boys just head through that gate thar, and you can hunt all day in that old pasture without gettin' lost much. That big cactus flat holds plenty of them little devils. Either you'll run into them or they'll run into y'awl. And ifin you stick one of them varmints, don't let 'em get to chewing on your leg. I sure hate to be wastin' the day gettin' some slick patched up in town. And whatever you do, don't you be crossin' no fences, especially that electric fence on the west line. I got my pet longhorns over there and they ain't quite used to slickers like y'awl."

"No problem," I assured him. "We don't care much for cows unless they're well-done and covered with lots of catsup." I winked at Toad. He returned his wide grin.

Lowering an unamused eyebrow, Joe reached his lanky arm across the cab of the truck and flicked open the door handle. "You boys better be gettin' to huntin' them pigs. I'll be back to check on ya around lunchtime. Remember, no crossing to them other pastures."

We got out and grabbed our bows. Joe spun the truck around and gave us a quick hand gesture. It looked somewhat like a wave so we waved back. He glanced in the rearview mirror and was still shaking his head as he disappeared among the mounds of cactus.

Toad and I wandered north into the sprawling ocean of prickly pear, soon accompanied by a pesky drizzle on the back of our necks. It wasn't long before the light rain turned the parched Texas dust into a sticky mess. The gumbo mud got so bad we couldn't take ten steps without stopping to kick free the massive globs clinging to our feet. It was like walking on freshly chewed bubble gum.

After several feeble hours of stumbling aimlessly through the mud and cactus, without so much as a pig track, we decided to call it a morning and headed back along the western fence toward the gate. A half mile from the gate, Toad, who was leading the way, stopped like he'd hit a brick wall. His eyes widened to the size of prickly pears and the hair on the back of his neck bristled like a javelina's.

As Toad eased forward with a nocked arrow, I spotted the focus of his trance-like stare. There, coiled next to a fencc post, laid a toad's worst nightmare, the biggest diamondback rattler I'd ever seen.

"What in the world do want to shoot that nasty thing for?" I asked. "Forget it, Toad, it's more trouble than it's worth."

Toad ignored me. His bulging green eyes were locked in a stare-down with the huge rattler. "I hate these things," he hissed, then unceremoniously drew his longbow and shot the snake just below its swaying head.

The diamondback coiled violently, snapping the cedar shaft and wiggling under a large patch of cactus just on the other side of the fence. After a few fleeting twitches, the huge rattler gave up its snake ghost.

"Great shot," I said, "but too bad ol' snake-eyes made it to the other side of Joe's hot fence."

Toad wheeled around, still wild-eyed, and stuck out his lower jaw. "There's not a fence around that's about to stop me from getting that diamondback! For years I've dreamt about arrowing one of them things and getting it mounted. And now he's just about mine."

I could see Toad was determined to display the great score he had righted for all the countless toads that had been eaten by rattlesnakes over the ages. There was no stopping him. Hesitantly, we approached the three strands of electrical wire. A nasty blue pulsating spark arched out from the lower strand where a blade of grass dared lean too close.

"ZAP!"

Toad eye-balled the fence for a minute then a sly toady grin swept across his face. "It's simple," he explained. "I'll just hop over this fence. It can't be much over three and a half feet high. Did it all the time when I was a kid. And by timing my jump between the sparking pulses, I'll be okay even if I do touch it for a second. It won't poke me."

Ol' Toad was a heck of a hopper alright, but that fence looked higher than his squat legs could clear.

"Poke hell!" I said. "By the size of the spark, I'd say Joe has this thing wired hot enough to knock one of his rangy longhorns into next week. That fence probably electrocuted every javelina around here. Matter of fact, we haven't seen a living thing within 200 yards of this fence."

"Go ahead, be a sissy," Toad said. "I'll get my snake. Just watch this."

Before I could say another word, Toad tossed me his longbow and sprung into action. His first hop faltered horribly. The mud and slippery footing caused him to slip and only make it halfway over. He landed with one leg on each side of the fence, the hot wire poised tight up between his legs. Toad frantically regained his footing and tensed his legs. He raised up on his toes, his eyes darting from me to the wire as if there was some way I might save him from the next second. The tension of that next second was as taut as that wire pressed against Toad's crotch. He prayed, I hoped, but we both knew it was coming, too quickly to escape. Our eyes settled on the wire at the same instant the giant spark finally pulsed.

What Toad lacked on that first jump, he more than made up for when the deadly blue spark snapped from the wire, striking the lone contact point. Toad shot into the air like a runaway Cruise missile, clearing the six-foot mark before dropping in a lazy arc. In an inverted belly-flop, he landed squarely on a clump of cactus waiting on the other side of the fence. He flattened the spiny mound of prickly pear with a resounding "plop!" then rolled in slow motion, face down in the mud.

I wanted to bust out laughing but in case he was dead I waited for him to show his face before I set in. But he didn't. In fact, he wasn't moving at all. I feared the worst, threw our bows over the fence, and hurdled the top wire. I rushed to Toad's side and rolled him over.

As I turned him over upright, his eyes suddenly tightened in pain and his mouth drew into a wide grimace. He made a terrible noise, half croak, half moan, then blinked his eyes.

"For cripes sake," I said, "you scared the tar outa me. I thought you croaked or something bad."

"I-I-It is something bad," he moaned. "You just rolled me over on a butt full of cactus spines and drove them in past their barbs. Ouchy, ouch. Get off me!"

Sure enough, I had unknowingly driven a big wad of spines even deeper into his hind quarters. His back quiver, however, had protected his back. The only other damage was to the feathered ends of his arrows. They had snapped cleanly when he hit the ground.

Unable to see or pull the spines himself, I had the delicate job of yanking the countless barbed stickers from his quivering flanks. It kind of reminded me of pulling porcupine quills from my old hound. But Ol' Blue never howled that loud.

"She loves me..."

"Ouch!"

"She loves me not."

"Ouch, damn it. Just hurry up."

After I plucked the spines from his hide, Toad pulled up his britches and hobbled over to his snake. It was a monstrous thing — a good five foot long and looked like it weighed 20 pounds. He admired the diamondback for a moment then stuffed it into his fanny pack.

"No way I'm going near that Gestapo fence again," Toad said, his legs bowed more than ever like he was riding an invisible horse. "I won't be able to sit for a week as it is. And as for my future love life — I'm afraid to even venture a guess. We'll just have to walk down the fence line until we reach the main gate. That's the only safe way out."

Toad's plan sounded like a good idea, and it probably would have worked. But one thing neither of us had counted on was Joe's longhorns. Like everything else in Texas, lone star cows are big. And Joe's longhorns looked like boxcars, mean ones. We first spotted them about a quarter mile from the gate — at least 30 of the beasts, casually chomping dried grass. They looked like they had all the arrogance and temperament of a herd of Cape buffalo, complete with horns that could kill in an instant. I had learned long ago that range cattle will do just about anything — mostly bad things. And this bunch looked like trouble in spades. I tried to mask my concern to give Toad a little confidence. Animals can tell when you're scared and Toad looked downright horrified.

"If we can make it to that line of mesquite trees," I said in a quivering whisper, "we just might slip past this herd of oversized Whoppers. Just stay cool and look nonchalant. We'll be fine."

His face now ashen with fear, Toad just nodded open-mouthed and followed me along the fence, his tongue flicking nervously in and out. We eased ahead like we were walking on egg shells as a seven-footer sauntered out of the cactus and locked a brown-eyed stare on us like radar. He looked as menacing as the six-foot horns gracing his ugly head. The big longhorn held his ground, giving us the meanest look I've ever seen from man or beast. Just as I thought we were about to make it, we routed a bedded calf that clambered to its feet, bawling its fool head off.

Instinctively, Toad and I froze. Then a sound like distant thunder rose into the mud-muffled pounding of a hundred hooves as the entire herd of head-wagging longhorns erupted from the brush, heading straight for us.

"Run for your life!"

We broke into a mad dash. I sprinted a hundred yards before I realized poor Toad was lagging pitifully behind. The combination of his electrocution, cactus jabbing, and the weight of that 20-pound snake flapping in his fanny pack, were taking their toll. The longhorns were gaining.

From the safety of the mesquite trees I yelled, "Drop your fanny pack, it's your only chance. They're almost on top of you!"

Wild-eyed and flying over clumps of cactus, Toad unbuckled his pack and flung it over his shoulder into the path of the oncoming cattle. The pack hit the ground with a "kerthump," Toad's shimmering prize spilling under the thundering herd. Tons of churning hooves instantly pulverized it into rattlesnake mush.

Dumping the pack gave Toad a short burst of speed, but it was all too short. The cattle overtook him 30 yards from the trees. I expected to see him impaled on one of those dagger-like horns at any moment, but they seemed hesitant to make the kill. Three huge longhorns cornered Toad between a nasty wall of cactus and the dreaded fence. With slow deliberate steps, they moved in on him, mouths drooling with thick slobber.

"If you've ever thought about saving someone's life," Toad shouted, "by God you better hurry, or you'll miss your chance — these crazy cattle look like man-eaters!"

My only arrows were tipped with broadheads, and I wasn't up to killing Joe's cattle — at least not yet. Frantically, I looked for rocks or a stick — anything. Then Toad let out a holler. The longhorns had backed him into the prickly pears, the thorns again biting into his tortured backside.

Then it dawned on me! I yanked an arrow from my quiver and quickly hacked off several hard prickly pears from the nearby cactus. Using my boot sole, I snapped the broadheads off three arrows and stuck each of the splintered ends into a spine-covered pear. Armed with my cactus-tipped longhorn busters, I crept toward Toad's anguished moans.

As I rose to shoot, I expected to see the worst, but the cattle were simply nibbling at Toad's new fleece camo jacket. One had a firm grip on a pocket while another pulled at his sleeve.

"Hurry up and do something, for heaven's sake," Toad gasped, "these damnedable creatures are about to eat me, piece by piece!"

I drew back my prickly pear missile just as the longhorns began tearing the pockets off Toad's jacket. I aimed for the meanest looking one and let 'er fly. The cactus-tipped arrow flew true, hitting the beast squarely in the flank. It let out a powerful bellow, spraying Toad with a nasty shower of cow saliva. The longhorn wheeled from the pain, startling its camo-munching comrades, and they thundered off into the brush. Like a scared rabbit, Toad dashed for the safety of the trees.

We didn't stop running until we cleared the gate at the far end of the pasture. Safely on the other side of the rusted gate, we both collapsed, panting wildly. Toad looked awful. He was covered with a slimy layer of cow spit and mud, and his new jacket was torn to shreds.

"Man, I was almost a goner," he wheezed, "Those cannibal longhorns just about had me for lunch."

Suddenly, a booming laugh exploded from the nearby brush as Joe stepped out slapping his thighs and shaking his head.

Red faced, Toad clambered to his feet. "It ain't no laughing matter, Joe. Your loco longhorns tried to kill me! If I hadn't broken my arrows, I'd have shot them overgrown T-bones."

Joe's laughing ebbed and he took on a serious look. "Well then, it's a damned good thing you did break your silly arrows, cause them cows of mine wouldn't hurt a flea."

"Not a flea he says?" Toad sputtered. "My God, look at my jacket. What do you call this?"

"I call that a hungry bunch of cattle," Joe said. "They've had a hard time this year because of the drought. Ain't enough good grass here to feed a rabbit. So I got to feed 'em grain cakes. And it's just about lunch time."

Joe opened the gate and cupped his hands to his mouth.

"Here, Lester. Here, Macky. Here, Stonewall, comey comey, come-on. Lunch time."

From the cactus came rumbling the entire herd of would-be man-eaters. I grabbed for a cactus-tipped arrow. Toad backed into the brush.

"Lower your cactus, son," Joe said. "Don't shoot. They're just a little hungry is all."

"Tell me about it," Toad said. "Some tried to eat me."

Joe shook his head as the longhorns pranced up to him with the delicateness of lambs and began sniffing the bulky pockets of his long jacket.

"I put the grain cakes in my pockets," he said, stroking a few of the longhorns. "It's kinda cute havin' them fish the cakes out. Been doin' it since they were calves. But it's not near as fun as watchin' them tear Toad's pockets clean off lookin' for cakes that ain't there."

He started laughing again and the cattle looked up at him then at Toad.

"All these babes wanted was their noon handout."

Joe lapsed back into his booming laugh. I joined in, and after a moment, a smile even crept across Toad's face. Finally the laughter trailed off. Joe sighed and strode next to me.

"Okay, boys," he said, his voice as hard as his face, "fun's over. Now just what in Sam hell were you two doin' in with my cattle — and howd ya get past that hot fence?"

While Toad winced and I searched for the right words, Joe pushed back his Stetson and crossed his arms. "I don't suppose you boys thought you'd find greener pastures on the other side of that hot fence? Well if you did, I can tell you damn straight; longhorns, javelina, and city-slick bowhunters always seem to think them pastures where they ain't are always greener than the ones they're in. Ifin there's one thing I've learned in this miserable life, it's that greener pastures only exist in the mind. And considerin' you boys obviously don't have a working one between ya, let's hear the real story."

So our story began, two greenhorns looking for greener pastures of sorts. Joe shook his head while we explained.

Toad fiddled with his ripped camo.

Nearby, the longhorns watched.

EL DIABLO'S OFFSPRING

Entranced by the dancing colors of the mesquite fire, I sat listening to the lonely song of a Texas coyote singing into the night. Across from me, slumped against a tree, my hunting partner, Toad, took another draw on a cold one, trying to unwind from a long day of roaming the cactus flats near the Mexican border.

A gust of wind roused the smoldering embers. I winced from the smoke and ash, and as I reopened my eyes, a hunched form materialized in the red glow near our fire.

"Buenos tardes, bowhunters," said a raspy voice. "I see you come for the javelina."

I was either too weary or stunned to speak. Toad, mouth agape, just stared. Before us, wavering in the wood smoke, a withered little man covered with coarse rags, peered from under his matt of white hair. He stretched a gnarled hand to brush my longbow hanging in the tree.

"Your bows are much like mine," he hissed. "So I will warn you. Do not go near the flint bluff. It is the playground of El Diablo."

Old Joe, our javelina guide, hadn't mentioned anything about a ragged caretaker or any character named Diablo. I cleared my throat.

"Sorry, old timer, but we don't know about this flint place or your buddy, Mr. Diablo. This is our first time here. You'll have to forgive us, we're just greenhorns. And we sure don't want any trouble."

He canted his neck like a buzzard and croaked, "Then trouble you should avoid, bowhunter. Years ago a hunter from my tribe disturbed the ancient spirits on the flint bluff. Then El Diablo cursed this land with a burning drought that scorched everything and consumed my people. The only creature to survive his wicked play was the bastard offspring of the javelina and cactus rabbit. And now El Diablo's offspring guards the spirits of my people."

Toad's nerves, sputtering like the fire, finally kicked in. "Whoa, time out, bub," he said, "we didn't fall off the potato wagon yesterday. We heard about you cactus snake-charmers preying on visiting hunters. We're not buying. But thanks for the show. We just came here to bowhunt and we're not about to —"

He was cut short by a hissing growl as the ragtag leaned over the fire's glow.

"I shall not warn you again, amigo. El Diablo is less forgiving than I."

The old man widened his wrinkled features, exposing the milky eyes of a blind man. His mouth contorted into a toothless grimace as a gust of wind swirled hot sparks around him. Toad and I turned our faces from the hot smoke, and when we looked back, the old man was gone. Only his woven sandal prints remained in the red dust.

Toad and I rubbed our eyes, squinting into the night for some sign of the old man. He had disappeared as mysteriously as he had come.

"What do you suppose that was all about?" Toad asked, turning to face the blackness of the night, backing closer to the fire.

"Maybe it was one of those boarder beggars who casts a curse on you then tries to milk you for a few bucks or a cold beer to make the spirits go away. How would I know? I'm just glad he's gone."

Toad scuffed a boot in the dust. "I know! It was probably that old fart, Joe, trying to get even with us for wandering among his prize longhorns the other day. He put the old man up to it. Probably paid him to scare the bejeezies out of us. That's the only thing that makes sense."

"You're right. Guess the only way to get Joe off our back is to let him think the old beggar really spooked us. He'll feel he's settled the score."

Toad and I crawled into the small tent and burrowed into our sleeping bags. We peered through the mesh door, watching the embers of the fire fade, white smoke drifting into the darkness as they died. Somewhere in the night a creature made an eerie cry. Toad fell asleep first. I watched for the beggar to reappear by the fire. He didn't. But he wandered among my dreams.

We were just finishing instant oatmeal and cocoa the next morning when old Joe rattled up in his pickup.

"Mornin', yanks," he drawled, fresh Red Man dribbling down his beard-stubbled chin.

Did he eat that stuff for breakfast?

"You dudes ready for some more javelina action?"

"Do cows make pies?" Toad said. "Of course we are. When it comes to bowhunting, my middle name is 'ready'. Let's go."

I smiled and Joe shook his head. Toad and I grabbed our bows and piled into the pickup.

Joe lurched his truck down the rocky two-track and began whetting our enthusiasm by telling us about likely javelina haunts.

"Matter of fact, I'll take you to one of my secret spots. Nobody's hunted it in years. The pigs really like it there; the old flint bluff."

Toad elbowed me in the ribs.

I looked at him and winked.

"Oh geez, not the bluff," Toad blurted in mock distress. "We were told not to go near there!"

Joe slammed on the brakes spinning the truck sideways in a dust cloud.

"Who in Sam hell told you that?"

"Why some little old man," I said. "Last night he told us some guy named Diablo wouldn't like it. Really scared us."

Toad nodded solemnly.

Joe took a healthy spit and gave us a hard look. But soon his penetrating stare began to melt into a grin.

"You boys pullin' my leg? I haven't heard that El Diablo yarn in over thirty years. It's one of the old Indian legends they used to spread around these parts. I don't know who in this world you were talkin' to, but there ain't no El Diablo unless you're wakin' up from a long Friday night courtship with a jug of moonshine. Musta been a cactus beggar pulling your chain last night."

"I don't know, Joe," I said, still playing the game. "That old guy really sounded like he meant business. Are you sure it's okay to go near this flint bluff?"

Toad raised a hand over his grin.

Joe popped the truck back into gear and roared through the cactus and mesquite-dotted landscape. "Of course it's okay to hunt there, you dang fools. What was you drinkin' last night anyway?" He gave us a side glance like we'd been chewing on loco weed for breakfast.

Finally he rolled the truck to a stop. "Thar she is, boys, your flint bluff. See, no evil spirits either. Just pigs and a few rabbits. Them javelina like to lay under that rock overhang. You can hunt your way back to camp, it's only about two miles."

As Joe turned the truck around, he paused, shaking his head with a laugh. "Oh yeah, if'n you boys see your buddy Ol' El Diablo, y'awl tell him I said howdy."

"Who's this Diablo anyway?" Toad asked him, faking his most worried toadish look.

"Why, 'El Diablo' is Spanish for 'The Devil'... You boys have a nice day."

Joe spat out the window and drove away, rocks and cactus spinning from under his tires. We waved good-bye.

"That guy ought to get into movies," Toad said. "He's an Oscar contender. Did you see the way he faked that surprise when we told him. I suppose he thinks he really got us good."

"That's fine by me," I said. "If we play this thing out 'til the end of the trip, maybe he'll spare us any more of his Texas pranks."

Toad nodded and without a word we began climbing the flint bluff, our longbows ready for the little desert pigs.

"Notice anything odd here, Toad?"

Toad stopped and looked around. "Awfully quiet, that's all."

"These Texas birds are usually singing their heads off in the morning down here. I don't even see any flying through the brush."

"Now that you mention it, it's kinda weird. Good thing we know Joe was spoofing us. Right? He was spoofing us?"

I shrugged my shoulders. "I guess." I hoped.

I had just jumped across a deep crevice in the rocks when I spotted an Indian arrow point laying in the dirt.

"Hey, Toad, check this out." As I reached for it, a sound like a distant hissing wind rose from the cactus. I spun toward the noise, dropping the point.

"What the hell's that?" Toad said, nocking an arrow and edging near.

The hissing faded like a dust devil losing its wind.

"I don't know. Maybe it's another snake." I swallowed and nocked an arrow.

Toad lowered his bow and shook his head. "Come on, it's probably just the morning wind. Looks like Joe's plan to spook you is working after all. Get real, don't be so gullible." Toad turned. "Cool, look, an arrow point."

Before I could say a word, Toad reached down and snatched the point. Immediately the hissing rose again from the nearby bluff. We spun, stood listening, unmoving. The hissing rose into a high-pitched scream punctuated by what sounded like the staccato gnashing of teeth.

"What the heck?"

A gray form emerged from a crevice and streaked through the brush, heading straight for us. It hugged the ground and moved so fluidly it looked like the shadow of a giant bird passing overhead. But then the brush moved. It wasn't a shadow, or a ghost either, and it was closing fast. Joe couldn't fake this. It had to be real. The old man's warning flashed; "the bastard offspring of the javelina and cactus rabbit."

"Quick, Toad, up that mesquite tree."

In three huge hops Toad was climbing the thorny branches of the lone tree. I glanced over my shoulder at the approaching thing and stumbled into a cactus, its spines sticking deep into my leg. I spun from the pain and fell on the loose flint. My bow and arrows scattered among the rocks. Wildly, I clambered toward the tree, the sharp flint slashing my shins and hands, more cactus spines piercing my legs. Suddenly the pain grew hotter and deeper, more wicked than nature should ever be. I turned and gasped. There, clinging to my leg, biting wildly, was El Diablo's offspring.

I kicked frantically and the creature went flying. It rolled in the flint, and turned to charge again. Coarse hair bristled along its back. Spittle flew from its fangs as it popped its jaws anew. It coiled to leap. From the tree, Toad's longbow twanged in the morning air. His arrow hissed back at the thing briefly before sounding with the unmistakable thump of arrow biting flesh. The creature spun out of control, like the cartoon character of the Tasmanian devil, snarling and biting at the arrow through its midsection. In seconds it lay still.

Limp and shaking, I rose to my feet. This had to be a dream, part of the old man's spell. Just wake up and it will all go away. I shook my head and blinked. The bad dream was reality.

Toad rushed to my side and helped steady me. Together we edged over to the thing.

"Joe wasn't in on this," Toad said, flatly. "This is unbelievable. Just look at that thing. It's really El Diablo's offspring."

I stood dumbly, nodding my head. Before us lay the small creature. It had the agile body of a rabbit and an oversized head like a javelina, complete with razor tusks. Its feet were a cross between hooves and claws, wicked and sharp like talons. The light shined off its coarse fur, a gray bristly coat with white tips on the fur like grizzly hide. It wasn't much bigger than a house cat, but looking at my leg, the thing could probably could have made short work of a deer, a man, or whatever the demon spirit in it wanted to claim.

"Holy smoke," Toad said, eyes bulging wider than usual, "that thing ripped your leg wide open. Man, we got to get you back to camp."

"Sure, but not without taking that thing with us. Nobody will believe a word of this without proof. Go ahead, Toad, stuff it in your day pack."

He reached down with the tip of his bow and nudged the thing into the top of his pack. "Pee-yew, it stinks like the dead. Geez, look at those tusks, incredible. Wait 'till Joe sees these."

"Tell me about them," I said, glancing down at my shredded blood-soaked pants. "They're genuine all right — real chompers. Now let's get outta here before any more of the offspring show up. And toss that arrow point away. I don't think we're supposed to take it."

By the time we hobbled back to camp the blood on my leg was crusted black. Even though it was starting to throb, Toad took a moment to empty the cooler and place the creature on ice.

"There, maybe it won't smell so bad when we bring Joe back here. Come on, let's get you to his ranch and get that leg patched up."

I didn't argue.We drove to Joe's ranch and his kindly wife, Ann, tended to my leg. It wasn't as bad as it looked. The fangs had pierced the flesh sideways under the skin making stinging but not serious wounds. When Joe saw that I was going to be okay, he tied into us.

"What in Godalmighty did you slicks get into now?" he bellowed. "If'n you don't have enough silly sense to keep your distance from those javelina, you're gunna hafta leave. I can't have my bowhunters gettin' chewed up like this, it's bad business!"

Toad's voice was firm but calm. "It wasn't a javelina. It was El Diablo's offspring. And I killed it with my longbow."

Ann dropped the box of Bandaids and gasped. Joe slowly pushed back his sweat-stained Stetson, clutching us in an icy stare.

"Show me," he demanded. "Now!"

We rushed back to camp. Toad lifted the top on the cooler and said, "You're not going to believe this, Joe, but now you can say 'Howdy' to the devil yourself."

Toad's mouth dropped as he looked into the now empty cooler. There, laying on the blood-stained ice was an Indian arrow point. Joe gave us a nasty look and then inspected the flint point.

"I don't know what in tarnation you slicks are up to, but I do know my arrow points. And this one here is mighty peculiar. There's no doubt about the style, it's over 1000 years old. But I'd swear it looks like it was made this mornin'."

Avoiding Joe's cold eyes, I glanced down, and there next to the cooler in the red dust were the unmistakable fresh prints of woven sandals.

LIPS

Cattails make a sorry campfire but I had no choice. They were the only thing for miles. I fed another handful to the fire. It billowed a brief puff before bursting into a flame that quickly crackled good-bye. Cattails. They burned liked they lived — fast and strong.

They stretched for miles up the coast of Lake Erie in both directions from my camp near Lookout Point, a small spit of sand jutting into the water. For most of the year it wasn't much more than a stopover for gulls. But now summer knocked at the door and the waters ran thick with carp. Each June I traveled to this remote stretch of shallows in search of a new world record carp. I didn't want lots. I only wanted one; the legend they called Lips.

From somewhere in the darkness, a small outboard broke the evening silence. Its guttural purr drew closer. Then the outline of a small boat materialized from the open water.

"Ahoy there!" a voice echoed from the boat. "Permission to come ashore."

"No permission needed, friend," I said, standing and peering into the night. "This here's state land, as much yours as it is mine."

The aluminum hull hissed as it grounded on the beach and the engine coughed into silence. A shadowy figure stepped out. Using a cane he limped into the fire's glow. Bending over the fire, he spread a half-toothed smile from under his shabby beard.

"Evenin', carper," he said, his mouth opening and closing with the rhythm of a carp sucking air. "Gibby's my name and carpin's my game. The marsh here says you been huntin' for the big one. Goin' on three summers it says."

"I didn't know the marsh talked."

"Oh, it talks plenty if you know how to listen." His mouth continued its odd cadence, the lower jaw dropping with each word. "But I suspect a city boy like you can't hear it. You have to live in it for years before it will even whisper to you for the first time. I've foraged in these cattails for twenty summers now and it tells me all I need to know."

"Really? Is there anything interesting this marsh here tells you these days?"

"Matter of fact, yeah. It says you're a man who would give just about anything to get a crack at Lips. And I just happen to be the only one who can guarantee you that crack."

I leaned forward and tossed a fresh handful of cattails into the fire. I looked away from the burst of flame, trying to hide the excitement in my eyes. How had he found me? Better yet, how did he know I was after Lips? Was it true? Was it more than just a legend?

"The marsh tells you true, Mr. Gibby. I am hunting for the giant they call Lips. But I don't know if I'm willing to give much to arrow him. And I might rather take him on my own. Besides, how do I know you could even locate something that's only a fable to most?"

"The name's Gibby," he snapped, his jaw suddenly more like a turtle than a carp. "Short for J.W. Gibson the third. And before you get too uppity you better take a look at this."

He reached up and snatched off his grubby cap and tossed it in my lap.

"So, what do you think about that, carper?"

I flipped it over in my hand. Nothing but a filthy brown baseball cap. "I think you need a fresh hat, Gibby. This one has seen better days." It also smelled like it had seen fresher ones.

"Cute, real cute. Look at it closely, city boy. Surely you're not that green about carpin'."

I turned the cap toward the fire's ebbing glow then threw more cattails into the flame. They surged into a blaze, casting a stark light on the old cap. Suddenly the realization hit me. The brim — the entire brim of his hat was made from a single carp scale. And it measured at least eight inches across. I sat there dumbfounded.

"No, it's not your legendary Lips," Gibby said. "But it's one of his kind. And there's plenty more like him if you're willin' to pay the price. I can have in you in the midst of them by sun up. Two hundred pounders, every one of them. And each wears lips the size of toilet seats. What do ya say, carper? Are you game?"

A thousand questions kaleidoscoped through my mind as I fingered the roughness of the massive scale. But in the end I knew only one mattered.

"What's your price, Gibby?"

"I knew you'd come around," he said, stroking his beard, his mouth now making slight sucking sounds with each drop of his jaw. "You've got that carpin' look in your eye, boy. No man hunts a legend for years without that special lure of the marsh in his blood. You sorta remind me of myself years ago, when the stories of Lips first started."

Gibby looked off into the night. "Most folks don't realize a carp can live fifty years or more, eatin' everything and anything it can wrap those lips around. Like beavers, they never stop growin' either. Lips probably got started young eatin' the biggest things he could suck down his gullet. Suppose he still does — geese, snapping turtles, other carp, whatever. Yep, I suspect Ol' Lips is as old as me. A living legend like that comes with a mighty high price tag. But I'll cut you a deal. Just five hundred bucks cash, no questions asked, and we do it my way. Understood?"

"Five hundred bucks? That's crazy. No fish is worth that much. Forget it. It can't be that big."

"Suit yourself, carper. Fact is, no tellin' how big he is now. Haven't seen him myself in three seasons. Nobody wanted him bad enough so I've left him alone. He may be a five-footer by now. Maybe more."

I rubbed the back of my neck and looked into the flames. Five feet? Heck, that was a hundred bucks a foot; a real bargain to get all that bowfishing fame, the world record, the only man to bag a legend.

"Okay," I said. I had to have that fish. And somehow Gibby knew it too.

"Fine then. I'll be here to pick you up two hours before sunup. Bring every fish arrow and extra reel you've got. And nothing but your heaviest bow. You'll need 'em."

"Two hours before sunup? My God. Carp don't even get active until late morning. Why don't we..."

"Like I said, carper, no questions or the deal's off! Two hours before sunrise. And have your money ready, cash."

He reached down with his cane and hooked the cap from my hands, donning it as he turned away. He took several steps toward his boat before stopping and glancing back.

"Don't think this is going to be any kind of picnic, carper," he said, tossing the cane near my feet. "Here, this will give you some idea of what you're up against tomorrow. I've seen damned good carpers turn to quivering marsh slime when they spotted one this size. So bring your nerve with you too, all of it."

Gibby hobbled into his boat and shoved off with an oar. His outboard putted to life on the first pull and he disappeared into the night. The darkness swallowed him as quickly as it had spit him ashore. Somewhere in the night a lone gull cried an eerie wail.

What clue did the cane offer? I picked it up and glided my hand over its three-foot ivory surface. Its smooth arch ended in a gnarled knob. Hmm, oddly familiar. Suddenly, the hair prickled up the back of my neck like a marsh crab under my cap. The cane was a giant rib bone from a carp! Must have been a five hundred pounder.

Huddled close to the cattail fire, I spent most of the night checking my gear and sharpening my arrows. Each time I seemed ready, I would look at the rib bone and feel the need to resharpen the tip on another fish point. The giant scale, the rib bone, the fish they must have come from made my 70-pound bow look puny.

Sometime in the night I finally drifted off to sleep. I rolled back and forth in the sand as if on heavy waves holding me afloat as dreams pulled me under into another realm. Gibby was there calling me, thrashing nearby in the dark water. I tried to help him but couldn't move. I watched as a giant carp wrapped its lips around his leg, sucking and working its huge lips. Gibby pounded its head with his fists, yelling, "carper, carper."

"Carper, carper. Wake up. It's daylight in the swamp. Let's get a move on. God, I thought you'd be ready."

I rubbed my eyes and sat up. Gibby picked up his cane and walked to the boat.

"Come on now. We've got a date with destiny. And destiny don't like delays."

I nodded and loaded my gear into the boat. We shoved off into the black water. I stuffed the five hundred bucks into his waiting hand. Gibby pocketed the wad and turned the boat straight out to open water then handed me a dirty burlap bag. It smelled of smoke and rotten fish.

"Looks like you could use some breakfast, carper. Got a treat for you in the bag."

I reached inside and pulled out a cold piece of flesh the size of a loaf of bread. It reeked.

"Go ahead. It's smoked carp. One of the choice big ones. Try it. It'll give you a marsh high, a real carp rush. I eat it all the time. It'll put lead in your pencil."

Gibby's eye's twinkled an odd glow in the moonlight. He belched and his face twisted into a smile, his mouth still working like a beached carp.

"Thanks, but I don't need any pencil lead. I'm not much of writer anyway. Besides, I'm not very hungry. Must be the anticipation."

"Suit yourself, carper. But the bag is for you too. One of my conditions. Put it over your head and don't take it off until I say. Got it?"

"Over my head? You're kidding? Why in—"

"Like I said, my way and no questions or the deal's off."

For a second I considered calling the whole thing off. But then I looked up at the cap on Gibby's head. I had to have one for myself — whatever it took. I donned the bag, dry heaving at the smell. Thank heaven for no breakfast.

We motored for over an hour, an occasional swell splashing over the low hull of his boat. The cool spray offered a little relief from the hot stench inside the bag. Finally, Gibby throttled back on the outboard and whispered into the bag. His breath reeked worse than the burlap.

"Listen careful, carper, lay down in the boat and not a peep out of you for the next hour. Keep still. And whatever you do, don't sit up in the boat. Try it and it may be the last thing you ever do."

I stiffened in the boat. What was going on here? Why all the mystery? And why had the old fart's tone taken on such a coldness? Damn, how had I gotten into this mess? Stuck out in the dark with a crazy old marsh rat. Was this really a carp hunt or was he going to take my money and dump my body in the muck for turtle bait? I sighed. Okay, just settle down. You've purchased your ticket with destiny. Now let's find out what it holds. Show a little backbone, man. The cold aluminum of the boat still sent chills creeping under my clothes.

Ten minutes later, Gibby killed the outboard and began rhythmically dipping the oars into the water. He showed uncommon power in his thin arms as I felt the boat surge forward with each pull of the oars. The only sound in the darkness was the gentle dripping of water off the oars between dips. He rowed for another half-hour before I sensed a stronger pull in his arms. A current fought his progress. Even through the hull I felt a gradual change in the water. The coolness gave way to a bath-like temperature. The inside of the bag grew more stifling.

"Okay, carper," hissed Gibby. "Time to earn your keep. Sit up and take your bag off."

I slowly rose and yanked the burlap from my head. I drew in a deep breath. The air smelled thick and heavy.

"You're alright, carper. Most guys would have turned back when I gave them the bag. You'll do just fine today. Don't you worry about nothin'. Ol' Gibby will take care of ya."

He grinned and patted me on the shoulder. I forced a half-smile and nodded. Maybe the worst was over. Then I looked up. Wrong. Before us in the gray light loomed a ten foot cyclone fence topped with barbed wire. A sign hung near the top of the fence. It was too dark to read. Gibby held on to a section of iron gate that hung from the bottom of the fence, spanning the twenty-foot flow of water around us.

"Wait just a second, Gibby. This doesn't look kosher to me. What's going on here?"

"No questions, remember? Besides, this is just the secret entrance to my carpin' spot. Ya don't think I'd make it easy for every city boy that comes along to sneak in here, do ya?"

His eyes showed the lie. I just shook my head. Was there any way all this could be worth it in the end? The gnawing in my gut made me wonder.

Using an oar, Gibby pried up a section of gate and began easing the bow of the boat under it. His arms quivered at the strain.

"Get with it, carper. Lend a hand. This gate's getting too damned heavy for an old marsh rat like me to muscle. Have some mercy on your elders for God's sakes."

I leaned forward in the boat and pushed up on the heavy section of gate. Slowly, we inched our way under. Past the gate, Gibby resumed rowing. The dark rings under his eyes looked deeper than before. Around us in gray twilight stood towering stands of cattails reaching skyward. They grew at least fifteen feet tall. I'd never seen bigger.

"Gibby, your leg. How did it happen?"

He stopped rowing, his mouth stopped making little circles.

"Never you mind about my leg. It happened a long time ago and knowing ain't going to help you none today, none at all."

Even in the dark his eyes probed mine as he continued dipping the oars. After rowing a hundred yards up the cattail lined channel, Gibby turned the boat into a small opening in the rushes. With one final grunt he pulled strongly on the oars and the boat nosed through the weeds then grounded against an embankment.

"Ride's over, carper. Time to portage. Just up and over this little dike here and we'll be in the pink of things. Just in time too. Sun's about to pop its pretty face in the east."

Gibby jumped out of the boat and began pulling on the bow even before I'd stepped ashore. I grabbed the gunwale and grunted as we skidded the small craft up and over a six-foot dike. At first, the other side looked like nothing more than a curtain of towering cattails. Then I spotted a small opening where Gibby had hacked away the thick growth. It revealed a faint glimmer of water. We pushed the boat into the water and climbed aboard. Gibby leaned forward in his seat, tipped back his cap, and peered into my eyes.

"This is it, carper. Get ready for the time of your life. You're about to enter carp heaven. No more than a handful of men have ever seen what you're about to witness. And most of them turned to goose droppings. You'd better get that bow of yours warmed up. When they're this big you don't get the luxury of makin' mistakes."

Gibby snickered as he pulled on the oars; a mad laugh like the wail of a gull.

The boat glided through the tunnel in the cattails and into open water. He pulled several more strokes before I looked up after double checking my gear. And there it loomed, bigger than life. Damn, we're in trouble. The giant domed structure and steaming twin cooling towers in the distance were unmistakable — Gravel Shoals Nuclear Power Plant.

"You old fool. You've got to be out of your mind to bring me here. Turn this boat around right now. You can keep the money. Just get me out of here, now. I demand it!"

Gibby shook his head and leaned back on the oars. "Easy, easy. Don't go gettin' all riled up, carper. This here's just one of their cooling ponds. My cousin works here and gives me special permission to hunt carp in it. Really. No sweat. Just wait until you see one. Lips the size of barrel staves."

"I don't want to see anything except my camp back at Lookout Point. Listen, I'll even throw in another hundred if you take me back before something bad happens. This water may be contaminated with radioactive stuff for all we know. That's probably how your prized carp got so ungodly huge. Think about it, man. This whole thing isn't right."

Gibby ignored my pleading and began nibbling on the stinking chunk of smoked carp. He smacked his lips and stared across the water toward the rising sun. His eyes narrowed into wrinkled slits.

"Better save your strength for what's about to happen. Cause one thing these big ol' bugle-mouths hate worse than anything else is being taunted with their own dead. They're usually more reclusive than an old swamp buck, but I discovered this one thing that drives them plumb loco, frothin' mad really. They come chargin' the boat every time. Gets downright ugly before it's over. Figured I'd give them an extra dose to really get them riled this time. Should cause at least five hundred bucks worth of action."

With that, Gibby dumped an entire bag of smoked carp chunks over the side. They sunk in the murky water, casting an oily film on the surface that began to grow.

"There, that ought to piss them off royally. Maybe ol' Lips won't be so shy now."

Gibby stood on the seat and steadied himself with an oar. Scanning the surrounding water with one hand shading his eyes, he looked like Captain Ahab on the eve of doom. His wrinkled features drew taut. His eyes widened and flashed. Gibby whirled and stabbed a finger across the water.

"Thar she blows, carper. Either get your bow a crankin' or hang onto something, cause we're about to get rammed!"

I wheeled in the boat and leveled my bow. At first I saw nothing; no splash, no tail, no form to shoot at — only a two-foot swell 50 yards out in the pond. Then I realized the swell was moving, growing, heading straight for the boat.

I began to draw my bow as the wake drew nearer. But as the dark outline streaking under the surface materialized into a nine-footer, my blood drained to my feet and I froze. I gasped for air but my lungs wouldn't budge. Gibby finally saw the size of the thing and dropped the oar. He lifted hands to a face gone white.

"Keeripes, it's huge," he said. "Never thought it would get that big, could get that big. Must weigh a ton. My God, this ain't good, not good at all. Quick, shoot the sonofabitch, carper, shoot it now!"

His frantic words sounded like faint echoes — a distant voice drowned by the drumming in my ears. Part of me screamed to draw, shoot, kill the thing, yet some greater part gripped me like an icy hand, tight and fast, not letting me wiggle. I stood unblinking, unmovable, a prisoner of carp fever, a spell, the awe of it all.

The crash of the leathery back striking the boat knocked me off my feet. I tried to break my fall but my head hit the corner of the outboard and for a moment I lay dazed in the back of the boat. Then Gibby's frenzied yells pulled me back from the brink of unconsciousness like my waking dream.

"Carper! Carper, help me. Don't let me end like this."

I pulled myself on the seat and looked around. Gibby was nowhere in sight. Finally my eyes focused on the head and arms thrashing in the water only a few yards from the boat. I strained over the gunwale, stretching to within a hand's grasp of his flailing arms.

"Stop thrashing. Grab ahold of me. Quick."

Gripped by panic, he struggled wildly, only sinking deeper in the water, his frantic gasps now a gurgle just under the surface. I made one final lunge and somehow managed to grab his shirt sleeve. I pulled. Gibby drifted to the side of the boat. He coughed out a mouthful of water then looked up. His face was ashen and drawn.

"God, get me out of this water, carper, now. I never figured it would be like this. We might handle a six-footer but not this thing."

I nodded and began pulling on his hands when it happened. Up from the murky depths they came. Like a gaping hole as they spread wider than the top of an oil drum — lips, heading straight for Gibby. The giant head rose almost clear of the water as the lips surged forward with a dreadful sucking sound. Gibby heard it too. I'll never forget his final look of surprise.

Like a massive vacuum, the carp sucked a hold of Gibby's back, then for a split second, rolled its deathly cold eyes up at me. They held a black hatred I had never seen before in any creature. Then, it gave one mighty jerk of its head, the lips tearing jacket and flesh as Gibby was ripped loose from my grip and pulled under. He managed only a child's squeal as he disappeared beneath the surface. His eyes never blinked as he went down out of sight, forever locked wide in disbelief.

I grabbed my bow and began screaming at the water as if somehow my shouts and anger could save him. But in the end there was no saving him. I scanned the murk for any sign of the old marsh rat. No bubbles, no blood, no tattered clothes floated to the surface. He vanished without a trace, the lips claiming all of him so completely as if he had never been part of the marsh. The only remains of J.W. Gibson III was his tattered cap floating next to the boat. I fished it out with an oar.

I don't remember how long I sat there dazed in the bottom of the boat, afraid to peek over the gunwale, trying to make some sense of it all. Lips never surfaced again, possibly content with its prize at the bottom. It was late afternoon when plant authorities discovered me floating near a water discharge and took me away — probably would have taken away my bow too, but I'd already thrown it overboard.

In the investigation that followed, I found out that Gibby did in fact have a cousin who once worked for plant security. He was fired years before for letting Gibby into the cooling pond. It turned out that the water wasn't contaminated with radioactive material. But it did contain a special flocculating agent designed to settle out to the bottom any isotope contaminants that might have been accidentally discharged. Carp being bottom feeders, ingested the stuff which strangely affected the growth portion of their pituitary gland. That, combined with the year-round tepid waters, caused them to grow beyond reality. Gibby was right. Two-hundred pounders, every one of them — except the legend they called Lips. God, the thing must have weighed a ton, even without Gibby inside it.

That day seems so long ago. Summer is just around the corner now. I reach up and take Gibby's cap off a peg near the door. Poor old bastard. I finger the brim and pull it on my head. I walk over to the refrigerator and take out a brown stained bag. I wander into my workshop and begin sharpening a new harpoon fish point I made. I set down the file and nibble on more smoked carp. Funny how a man's tastes change. I hold the point up to the light, its profile sharp and wicked. Yeah, maybe this thing driven from my new 90-pound bow will stop Lips this time. I'm sure I won't freeze up again. I'm just sure of it.

WHITETAIL DESPERADOS

We never should have tried it. It seemed innocent at the time, not much more than a devilish smart idea.

It all began as big Max and I huddled near the smoldering remains of our fire, the logs hissing a solemn tune during the final bowhunting weekend. Around us, ghostly shadows of leafbare trees danced outside the fire's glow, reminding us this was our fleeting chance to outwit a buck. Season was at an end. And we were desperate.

Although we tried throughout the season to imitate the whitetail sleuths we had read about in bowhunting magazines, Max and I had yet to even draw an arrow, much less blood. There was no denying it. We were less-than-average bowhunters, not even as smart as the yearling bucks that easily eluded our setups.

If necessity is the mother of invention, then a bowhunter's desperation might be the father of genius. Our genius of a hunting plan was spawned from the marriage of two ideas. By themselves they had been laughable failures, but when combined? Staring into the pulsating glow of the coals and pondering our failing reputations as bowhunters, Max unknowingly sparked the idea.

"I just can't figure," he said, sipping his tea. "That Estrous Euphoria deer lure I've been using drives bucks crazy when there's another deer around. But when a buck comes in alone, he gets spooky and always circles downwind, picking up my scent. Man, if there was only some way to convince him a genuine hot doe was waiting for him."

"I can't figure them either," I said. "My deer decoy brings bucks in on the run until they get downwind and smell it's not for real. If I could only make their noses believe she was the real thing."

Then, like flint striking steel, the two thoughts sparked as one. Our eyes widened in unison.

"That's it!" I gasped.

"Perfect!" Max blurted. "It's got to work."

The next morning under the cover of darkness, Max and I carried my doe decoy and his bottle of Estrous Euphoria to the hottest buck crossing in the woods. We set up the decoy near a fresh scrape, then Max pinned a cotton ball on her rump, dousing it with his Estrous urine. Finished, we stood there in the fast growing twilight admiring our seductive sweetheart, grinning at our combined whitetail genius. She was the perfect temptress.

Suddenly, we heard the distant grunt of an approaching buck. We scrambled for the tree stand, revealing the flaw in our plan — two desperate bowhunters, only one stand.

At that moment desperation overshadowed etiquette and friendship. I scurried past the lumbering Max, making it to the tree first. I was up the third step when Max grabbed my leg and pulled himself up. Kicking, I fought for position but he clawed past me, his oversized feet mashing my hands on branches and steps. The ruckus didn't bother the buck. If anything, it picked up its pace when it mistook my groans for the grunting of another buck.

Just as I pushed my way into the small stand with Max, the buck hit the Estrus Euphoria scent stream 50 yards away and began zeroing in on our temptress like a heat-seeking missile. Max fumbled for an arrow. So did I.

Nudging elbows and shoulders, we bartered for position on the stand. It proved a short contest. The buck no sooner hit the clearing when Max's face twisted into his now-you're-going-to-pay look and he drew. His draw stopped halfway when his brawny elbow landed squarely in my eye socket. The unexpected bump triggered his release, sending me off the back of the stand and his arrow harmlessly short.

I was still clenching my bow when the safety belt snapped tight with the twang of a bass fiddle. It squeezed a panicked scream out of me that probably sent every squirrel, chick-a-dee, and deer within a half mile into the next county — our duped buck included.

For the next half-hour Max grumbled about me messing up his shot. He obviously thought that his little bottle of buck lure was more important than my much larger decoy. By the time we finished arguing who was going to shoot next and who was going to cling to the back side of the tree, the morning sun burned high in a cloudless sky and the only deer left in the woods was our decoy temptress. We headed back to camp

Okay, so our genius had a flaw. Nothing we couldn't remedy.

"Let's settle this a man's way," Max said back in camp, his eyes more desperate than ever.

"What? Best two out of three arrows at the practice target?"

"Naw," he said, "was thinkin' more like arm wrestling."

He began rolling up his sleeves, exposing tree-trunk arms.

"Come on, Max. That's not fair. Let's just toss a coin."

Before he could protest I flipped a nickel into the air.

"Call it," I said.

"Tails!"

"Sorry, you lose. See, heads."

"How about a bowhunter toss?" he said, reaching for me.

I ducked and grabbed my bow.

"Man, you are desperate. I'm heading for the stand. You'll get your chance tomorrow."

I left. Max sulked.

Tiptoeing through the woods, I was surprised to discover that our temptress had been knocked over. She was laying on her side and the cotton ball was missing. Ummm... the obvious work of an overaroused buck. This could be good, very good. I righted the decoy and scented up a new cotton ball with Max's buck lure. Okay, lover-boy, anybody for seconds?

It wasn't long before hooves churned through the leaves in my direction. The flicker of antlers and legs appeared, circling downwind. Darn. The buck eventually picked up my scent then snuck off. Was probably pissed that some hunter captured its receptive doe and tied her up near its tree. It even appeared to glare over its shoulder as it disappeared into the thicket.

That evening around the campfire I told Max about the foul up.

"It's like he knew I was there, Max. Oh, he wanted that decoy alright. Probably waited for me to leave then went back and nailed her again. What do you bet?"

"I bet he don't get a second chance when I'm sitting there tomorrow morning. Just let him try."

The following morning Max crept into the ambush to again find the temptress laying on her side, cotton ball missing. He rebaited her with a fresh scented cotton then climbed into the stand. As if replaying the game to perfection, the buck soon appeared then circled downwind of Max. The buck gave him a nasty look after catching his scent. It tore up some saplings in frustration before again melting into the thicket. Max left the stand more desperate than ever.

Okay, this was it. We were down to our final evening of the hunt. Season would be over in a matter of hours. With desperation running deep in our bloodshot eyes, we gazed into the afternoon campfire. I prodded it with a stick. Sparks rose into the air.

"If there was only some way to make him stay interested in the decoy when we're not there," I said, "maybe we could sneak up on him for a shot. Something to really hold his attention."

Max's eyes widened. "Yeah, grab a hold of his attention and keep him there. That's the ticket."

He rose to his feet, an odd grin showing under his beard. Max dashed to his pickup and began rummaging under the seat. He pulled out a pile of empty pop cans, rags, broken arrows, a roll of wire, and finally a rusty muskrat trap.

"Max, have you lost your marbles? Muskrats don't have horns. And you sure can't leg-hold trap a whitetail."

"Ain't going to try and leg-hold trap him. I just want to grab the end of his attention for a while."

"What?"

"Come on and watch. You'll get the idea."

Max tucked the trap under his arm, grabbed the roll of wire, a wad of cotton, and his bottle of Estrous Euphoria before heading toward the decoy. I followed. As we neared the decoy, Max began fingering the trap and chuckling.

"Come on, Max, that buck will never step into that little trap."

His grin widened into a jack-o'-lantern smile. "He ain't gonna *step* into it!"

Max wrapped both jaws of the trap with cotton then wired it to the rear-end of the decoy. Still chuckling, he gingerly set the trap and soaked the cotton with buck lure.

"Oh Man," I said, a nervous grin tugging the corner of my mouth. "You're the nastiest deer hunter I've ever seen. Gosh, Max, do you really think we ought to try this? I mean is it legal?"

"Legal smeagle, who cares? We only have one evening left. I'll try anything to catch that buck sneaking in here to play lover boy again with our decoy. He's made a fool out of me for the last time."

I rubbed my chin. Maybe he's right. No one will know. Besides, it might be neat if this thing really works. Just think, we could get whopper bucks every year, become famous bowhunters in no time. Cool.

Max propped his hands on his hips, smiling at his creation.

"Too bad we won't be here to see the expression on his face when that trap grabs him. Man, what a show that would be. Be worth a million bucks. But we better hide on the other side of that ridge until we hear him struggling in the trap. Then we'll run over and stick him."

With that, Max stood on his tiptoes behind the trap to be sure it was wired at the right height to catch the buck in "the act." I leaned around to look.

Neither of us heard the buck sneaking in close behind us.

But we sure heard his snort.

It echoed through the woods.

I jumped and spun at the sound, bumping into Max who was already off balance. He fell forward, windmilling his arms helplessly as my nudge pushed him toward the waiting trap.

For a rusty old trap it sure had a hair trigger. Strong jaws too. The front of Max's pants no sooner brushed the spring plate when the jaws snapped. Even through the cotton and layers of clothing came the sharp sound of trap biting groin. An instant later big Max roared with pain, eyes wide in surprise. Gripping the trap in both hands, his momentum carried him further until finally he and the temptress fell in slow motion, like two chopped trees tumbling into the leaves.

It took longer than it should have to run back to the truck, find the clippers, run back, and snip Max and the trap free from the decoy. He had somehow wired the thing so it couldn't be sprung open without removing it completely. Must have been his ace in the hole so the buck couldn't get away. God, I would have never imagined that a man in that much pain could thrash so violently for so long. When I finally opened the trap's jaws, Max curled up into the leaves and sobbed.

Later at the hospital, the nurses managed to stop giggling long enough to give Max a tetanus shot and bandage up his wounds. Nothing was severed and the cotton wrapping on the trap had at least saved him from needing stitches. Finally, he scraped up the last of his dignity and hobbled out the door.

We didn't say much during the long drive back from hunting camp. Max just gazed out the window, eyes flat, face sullen.

We never hunted together after that. I like to think that the ordeal changed Max, made him less desperate as a deer hunter. It sure changed me.

Since then I don't use decoys, lures, or any of the other gimmicks that line the shelves of archery shops, preying upon the inherent desperation in so many deer hunters. I learned long ago that a bowhunter's desperation can be the father of genius — sometimes a wicked one.

I also learned that a genuine bowhunter doesn't give in to desperation, he turns it into determination. And that will ultimately make him more successful than the most ruthless of whitetail desperados.

Every time. Guaranteed.

LESS OR MORE

Wes Sommers turned the tractor into the last row of standing corn. Clattering beside him, a single-row corn picker stripped ears from the parched stalks. Wes smiled as he neared the end of the row. Three acres of stunted corn wasn't much of a crop, he thought, even for a weekend farmer. But the local deer would welcome the nourishing handout when winter's bite gnawed at their ribs.

Still grinning, he noticed an ear of corn stuck near the top of the picker where the steel teeth drew them in. He reached over with his left hand and gave it an idle swat. The teeth grabbed the ear. And much to his surprise, they grabbed his gloved hand along with it.

Time ebbed into slow-motion for Wes, etching a surreal scene in his mind that would follow him the rest of his days; the cool steel teeth chewing away his fingers, threatening to draw him arm and all into its corn-eating maw. Oddly he felt little pain, only rage at the thing gobbling his fingers and the unfair tug of war over impossibly stretched tendons. Then came the mighty snap when they finally tore, sending him cartwheeling off the tractor into the stubble.

Surgeons mended the mess as best they could, using the flap of shredded hand to wrap over what remained of the palm. The only digit to survive the ordeal was the little finger. At least fate left him with something to pick his nose, he thought as he watched them bandage the stub. He also realized with sudden clarity that his life as a wood carver was over. Then a more devastating realization surfaced through the fuzz of sedation; the three fingers and thumb that had held his bow rock-steady for decades now caked the corn picker's teeth in a rusty smear of brown.

For the next week Wes stared out the window from his hospital bed watching the blaze leaves of a lone maple drop to the lawn. He saw each fallen leaf as a day of bowhunting lost forever, a day he should have been in the woods embracing his passion in life. Finally the tree stood as bare as his stub, a bleak thing without a hint of promise. But at least the tree would sprout new leaves in spring. He left the hospital with shoulders slumped, a flat gaze in his eyes.

In the months that followed, the stub healed into a gristly mass of purple tissue. But the nerves once leading to strong fingers refused to mend and tormented Wes with ghost pains that took his breath away. Any dramatic temperature change — the morning shower, washing his hand-and-a-half before dinner, handling a glass of ice tea — sent ghost pains ripping up his arm as if the fingers were still attached and being torn away again. Wes built up powerful jaw muscles gritting his teeth against the pain and worried if he would ever be free of the haunting spirits. The doctors said not to worry though, everything mends with time.

Wes believed them and began fashioning a new handle on his bow to accommodate his partial hand. Another month of healing passed before he tried his new handle; a socket to fit his stub, crudely carved from birch. He slid his stub into it, the cool tingle of the wood sending a pulse of pain up his arm.

"Damn you, fingers," he cursed under his breath. "You're gone, give it up, let me get on with my life."

He gritted and drew tension on the string. He shuddered at the pain. Tears welled in his eyes. Okay, maybe not today. We'll try again. Yeah, maybe tomorrow.

Three month's worth of tomorrows passed yet Wes still couldn't draw the bow. The few times he overcame the pain of the handle's socket pressing against his stub, his wrist or forearm collapsed. The picker had claimed more than fingers and thumb. It had left him with atrophied muscles, fused tendons and damaged nerves. One failure led to another, and eventually, Wes gave in to the unrelenting pain of trying with his useless stub. Finally, he abandoned his dream of bowhunting again, just a fool's fallacy. He slipped his bow inside its case and stuffed it in the rafters of his workshop. No sense seeing it all the time if he couldn't shoot it. Forget it, man. Accept it, move on.

Wes tried to move on with his life, but by early summer he sank into despair, a normal reaction his doctor said. Out of work and out of hope, he shut out the world, drawing back into daydreams of seasons past where his arms worked true and strong climbing tree stands, shooting arrows and dragging bucks. One afternoon while lost in the forest of his dreams, fate again stepped into Wes' life. Skip, his one-time brother-in-law, stopped by.

"Hey, Wessy, long time no see," Skip said as he bulled his way past the screen door. "Heard about your hand from one of the guys at the club. Said you couldn't shoot no more."

Wes shrugged, searching for some excuse to get rid of Skip. Instinctively, he slid his stub into his pocket, but not before Skip's eyes locked on it.

"Wheweee," Skip bellowed. "The guys were right, that thing sure trimmed you back a notch. No wonder you can't shoot your bow. Crap, it hurts me to even look at the thing. Must be a bitch tying your shoes."

Color rose into Wes' cheeks. He bunched his right hand.

"Come on, Wessy, lighten up. I know we weren't the best of friends even when I was married to your sister. But us handicapped guys, we got to stick together."

Wes' eyes darted to Skip's hands, counting fingers, checking for thumbs.

"Naw, it ain't nothing like that mess of yours. Got this thing called carpel tunnel syndrome. Makes the fingers stiff in my left hand once in a while, usually the day after golfing. So I told my doc I shot my bow left-handed and had trouble holding the string. He never blinked twice. Gave me a note so I can shoot a crossbow during bow season. Neat crap, huh? I'd have gotten that note years ago if I'd known how much easier I could shoot that thing than my bow. You're a shooin with that wrecked hand of yours."

Wes' cheeks flushed anew at the mention of crossbows. He had seen a few crossbow guys in the woods over the years and cussed each time he saw one perched in a tree with their scoped contraptions. He never understood why those killing machines should be allowed in the woods during bow season, handicapped or not, crossbows weren't bows. They looked and shot more like guns.

But then Wes had never experienced the despair of wanting to bowhunt so desperately and not being able. The pain and frustration of grappling one-handed in life had a way of numbing perception. His features softened. One eyebrow raised. "How does the thing shoot?" he asked flatly.

"Wait 'til you see, man," Skip said as he grabbed Wes by the arm and headed out the door.

Skip led the way to his pickup and fished out crossbow and a handful of bolts. "Get ready for a blast, Wessy. Man, it's a scream zipping them with this thing," he said, cocking and shouldering the crossbow — with two able hands, Wes noticed.

"Go ahead, give 'er a try," Skip said as he slipped a bolt on the string and motioned toward the old practice bale near the garage.

Tentatively, Wes took the crossbow. After measuring its bulky weight with his good hand, he steadied it with his stub under the crossbow's forearm. He pressed his cheek into the ugliness of the thing and squeezed off a shot. The bolt smacked the bale with a thud.

"See, what did I tell you? Shoots like a demon, don't it? Welcome to the deer-slaying club, bro. Pretty soon you'll be kicking the ass of more bucks with one of these than you ever did with two good hands and a bow."

Wes looked down at the monstrous thing in his hand — a cold conglomeration of metal. The weight of its forearm pressed on his stub, its coldness triggering a ghost pain. The steel teeth of the corn picker again began chewing off fingers that weren't there. The memory flooded back. No, give me my hand back. Don't take it. Wes jerked away his stub and stumbled backwards, the crossbow clattering to the gravel near his feet.

"Hey, man, careful. I had to sell my compound and old recurves to buy that. That's a precision machine. Wow, what the hell's wrong with you?"

Skip's last words kept ringing in Wes' ears as he gritted his teeth at the pain. Yeah, what is wrong with me? Good question. Why are you doing this, trying this thing? It's just a glorified prosthesis. Can't you see that? His eyes flicked back to Skip, seeing him clearer than ever. He kicked the crossbow across the driveway toward Skip.

Skip jumped back. "Crap, are you crazy or just an asshole?"

"Neither. And nothing's wrong with me, fortunately. Just lost sight of things for a second, that's all." He looked at the crossbow and shook his head. "If that's what it takes to be part of your club, I'm not interested in joining. And I'm not interested in killing more deer."

Wes' eyes kept flicking back and forth from Skip to the crossbow, his mind leaping hurdles. The pull of a trigger to kill more deer; is that what bowhunting is coming to? Maybe for this jerk but not me. I've spent my life becoming a better bowhunter. I'm not about to go the other way because of this. His eyes dropped to the stub clenched in his good hand — one damned good hand.

Skip reached down for the crossbow.

"Take your toy and beat it, Skip. And keep on skipping all the things in life that take a little dedication, like bowhunting, marriage, you know the list better than most, Skippy."

"I should have known better," Skip said as he stormed over to the bale to pull the bolt. "Go ahead, try keeping up that tight-assed bowhunter's image you've wrapped yourself in for so many years. See where it gets you now. You can't even wipe your ass let alone shoot a bow. You ain't that high-falootin bowhunter no more. Just take a look at yourself. You ain't nothin' special no more, only some sore loser with a bum hand and a fat head."

Skip climbed into his pickup and slammed the door. "And when you fall off your high horse some day," he continued out the window, "don't come beggin' to me to show you how to kill deer with a crossbow. 'Cause it ain't gonna happen, Mr. Has Been."

Wes reached his good hand through the window and grabbed a shirt-full of Skip, yanking him roughly to the door. Skip struggled with both hands but couldn't break Wes' iron grip.

"Don't worry, Skippy, I won't come begging. I'm not interested in becoming more of a deer killer. And I'm sure not interested in becoming anything like you."

Wes released his grip and several popped buttons fell into Skip's lap. Skip twisted his face and dropped his pickup into gear, gravel flying from under the tires.

"And if I ever see your doctor," Wes hollered, as Skip drove away, "I'm telling him you're a right-handed liar. But maybe he'll still give you a note for having ham-strung integrity. Yeah, tell him you're mentally handicapped, maybe you can get a note for that."

As Skip drove out of sight, Wes smiled. God, it felt good to grab a hold of that weasel. He held up his right hand and flexed it. Didn't know it had gotten so strong — maybe strong enough to...

Wes marched into the house and gathered up his three right-handed bows. He drove to the local archery shop where he traded them for a left-handed model 20 pounds less than his usual draw weight. The shop owner also helped fit Wes with a release aid on a wrist sling, the man demonstrating a casual air as if he fitted archers with shooting problems every day. In a way he did, Wes thought, and he left the shop carrying his chin higher than it had been in months. If Skip can live with a left-handed lie, maybe I can live with the left-handed truth.

For the next three weeks Wes struggled to switch to left-handed shooting. Each time he drew, pressure from the wrist sling caused his mangled hand to swell blue with blood, the throbbing pain bringing sweat to his brow and watering his vision. He cussed his awkwardness when nocking an arrow and aiming, but smiled the first time his little finger finally found the release and the arrow leaped from the string.

With each passing day, gripping the bow in his right hand became more familiar. With each week, the muscles in his arms and partial hand found new strength. With each month the throbbing ebbed, the searing ghost pains dulled and the arrows grouped tighter. By October Wes was ready.

In his first few weeks afield Wes faced more hunting challenges than he had in decades. Unable to climb and hang a tree stand safely with one hand, he hunted from ground blinds. But the deer easily spotted him or picked up his scent. He added more brush and logs but it didn't take long before the deer began avoiding his ambushes altogether. The more he hunted, the fewer deer he saw.

Now a veteran to the brassy taste of challenge, Wes faced this setback as a fresh obstacle. He knew his hands could do their job, now he put his brain to working overtime too. He began to scout like never before, spending dawn 'til dusk roaming the woods. Each time he saw a new piece of the puzzle, his mind searched new realms for the answers. He began to read the faint impressions in the leaves as the passing of deer: certain bucks, cautious does, the reckless scamperings of fawns. Rubs that had once been just the markings of bucks became sign posts of information; the buck's travel pattern, time of day it rubbed, rack spread, height of tines, body size, age class, temperament — Wes' mind explored more possibilities than he had ever imagined from each fragment of deer sign.

As October faded into November's rut, Wes discovered heavy rut sign in areas he had never thought to scout before. He began to drift with the changing patterns of the deer, becoming a nomad, shifting locations daily with the flow of the herd. He abandoned his blinds and began to blend with the surroundings, melting into the shadows of deadfalls or vine clusters, sitting owl-still as deer neared. Becoming part of the forest, he marveled at the simple complexity of the whitetail's existence. Why hadn't I realized any of this before? Was hunting from a tree stand that different?

Despite all his intimate encounters with deer, Wes ended the early season without releasing an arrow. He had passed up good shots awaiting the perfect one. He had grown to love the deer too much to settle for anything less, especially with the lighter-weight bow and new form. My time will come. Patience is but a blessing to learn more about them, about me.

During the idle weeks of gun season, Wes still practiced shooting his bow. And for the first time in over a year, he wandered into his wood carving shop. He looked at the mallet on the bench. Go ahead, pick it up. You can't do what you don't try. He picked up the mallet. He turned it in the talon grip of his hand. Why did it feel so light, so delicate? He reached for a chisel with his stub, the little finger wrapping around its neck like the first coil of a snake, the handle pressing into the wad of flesh. He turned to an osage stump on the carving block. What was I going to make from this? A bowl, a lamp, maybe a napkin holder? He stood transfixed, staring at the irregularities in the grain, the lumpy places branches once grew. Who planted you, tree? How old are you? What marvels did you see in your time? What hidden wonder still lives in your stub?

Wes raised chisel and swung the mallet. Bits of osage flew. He swung again. His eyes narrowed, then widened. He swung harder, faster; and long into the night the chips of osage piled around his feet. Before dawn he finally dropped the tools on the edge of the block and kneeled next to his creation: the transforming image of a butterfly escaping its cocoon, the curling abstract wings revealing every hidden swirl of grain within the stump. Wes pressed his stub to his lips. He looked at the pile of stumps in the corner; oak, ash, cedar. There was so much beauty in them waiting to be set free. Why hadn't I seen it before? He held out his stub and smiled. Guess I have you to thank for this. The little finger rose to attention. I suppose now you know you just can't sit around picking my nose anymore. Wes laughed until tears filled his eyes.

December swept in raw and white as a big northwester blew in a foot of snow. Attuned to every detail of the changing season, Wes smiled at the challenge. He donned snow camo and pulled on mittens; the left one sewn to half-size with a hole cut for his little finger.

Wes now knew harsh weather would bunch the deer along an alder swamp east of a big oak ridge. He circled along the southeast edge of the swamp and found fresh tracks where hardwoods met the swamp — bucks scent-checking for does coming into their late estrus. A faint grunt sounded from up ahead. Wes nocked an arrow.

From out of the white maze loped a yearling doe, tail tucked, ears flattened. A small buck dogged her every move. Wes readied for the shot. The deer passed at 25 yards, just beyond his limit. They disappeared as quickly as they came. Wes nodded. She will return to the herd for safety. And she will likely use the same trail, hoping to shake the buck. He slipped within 12 yards of the scuffed tracks and crouched behind a deadfall. Minutes later the sound of hooves thumping frozen earth grew louder.

Time ebbed into slow-motion, etching a vivid scene that would follow Wes to the end of his days: the doe skipping along in her worried pose, the buck, neck outstretched in blissful pursuit. Wes drew. They neared. He grunted as the buck slowed. It stopped. The little finger moved with the purpose of three. The arrow bit cold air then hide.

Wes was sure of the hit, more sure than he had been of dozens of others over the years. Still, he waited 20 minutes before following the unmistakable trail.

As Wes crested the oak ridge, he looked up from crimson flecks in the snow and spotted the trail's end. There lay his deer under a canopy of vines. He nocked an arrow and walked slowly toward the fallen whitetail, the snow crunching loudly under his feet, the crisp air stinging his nostrils.

No need for the arrow. The deer lay motionless, a thread of steam rising from the slit behind its shoulder. Wes knelt beside the buck and gently lifted its head, counting five points on the diminutive rack. He stroked its neck and laid the head back down. He swallowed hard as his eyes drifted to his stub of a hand, the little finger poking from the mitten like a curious chipmunk from its burrow.

He dragged the buck from under the vines into a patch of morning sunlight. He took off his mittens, drew his knife, and opened the deer's underbelly. With both hands he reached deep inside its warmth. The wet heat flooded life into his right hand, but an instant later it sent searing ghost pain through his left.

Wes gasped as he jerked his hands from the deer, blood spotting the snow in a wide arc. He gripped his wrist hoping to strangle the pain but the numbing air only made it worse. He gritted his teeth. Go ahead, remind me of all I've lost. The pain began to dull from the blur of fingers being torn to a steely tingle he had grown to accept. He sighed. He looked at the stub, the little finger still twitching from the tingle. Wes smiled and nodded. Too bad your buddies aren't around to see how we have grown together, what we have done. He looked back at the deer. He reached inside it. His jaws bunched again. Go ahead, remind me of all I've become too.

He smiled and continued dressing the buck.

The morning sun had never shined brighter.

The Early Ones draws on chapters from Dan's acclaimed book, ***Traditional Bowyers of America.*** *This historical piece summarizes the foundation of our primitive roots in bowhunting.*

THE EARLY ONES

A rustle from the brush sent the two boys diving among the rocks near the creek. It was a poor place to hide, but circumstance gave them little choice. Their naked bodies were covered with red dust clinging to the sweat-lined wrinkles around their frightened eyes. Neither dared breathe as the padded footfalls approached.

Straining, in slow snakelike movements, the boys contorted bronzed bodies to conform to crevices in the rocks. Their brown eyes met, wide with fear before a menacing shadow darkened their faces as it paused near their hiding place.

Like their little brother the rock lizard, the boys squinted slowly and stopped all outward expression of life. Tightened stomachs ached as they breathed in harmony with the distant floating clouds. To become one with the lifeless red rocks was their only hope.

Soon, the feared one resumed her steady pace up the narrow trail to the woods. She was carrying her wood gathering harness and water skin. Today, they would be safe. The boys emerged from the rocks, grinning in triumph, and continued down the path to the base of the great cliff.

The feared one was Uni-na, the crazy hag. Her withered face held deep-set eyes that could cast a curse on a child. The evil spirits that haunted the distant singing caves sometimes traveled on the north winds and entered the old woman's head, sending her into a rage. When touched by these spirits, she wandered about casting evil curses on children reckless enough to get caught in her path.

The adults in the village paid little attention to her odd notions. They knew she was the harmless crazy one. The children, however, ran wild-eyed into the hills, hiding until the old woman tired and wandered back to her hut near the overhang of the great cliff.

Uni-na was forced to live there, isolated from the rest of the village, where her crazy antics wouldn't disrupt the tribe. Even though she was struck by the spirits, the crazy one could not be banished altogether. She was the woman of the tribe's creator of man-nee, Chu-no-wa-yahi, the crafter of the bow.

Like graceful deer, the boys bounded down the trail to the base of the great cliff where the bowmaker lived. There, squatting next to a smoldering morning fire, the old man stirred the embers. The boys saw past the ragged furs, matted grey hair, and leathery skin draped over the hunched pile of bones. In their eyes he was the mighty warrior Chu-no-wa-yahi.

From the corner of an eye the old man saw the boys approaching, but ignored them and began a low guttural chant while he continued working on an unborn bow. The boys knew the chant was the old warrior's special way of greeting them. Even though he cherished their bright faces near his fire, the old bowmaker was too proud to openly greet them. With eyes full of admiration, the two slowly crept near the fire pit, kneeling in the reddish dust near the old man.

When his audience settled, the bowmaker's chant turned into the broken song of an ancient tribal tale. Chu-no-wa-yahi's story was of the great hunter Yano-ni-yahi, who discovered the hidden valley of the white deer. As his quivering, rhythmic song entranced the boys, Chu-no-wa-yahi continued crafting the bow cradled over his shoulder. Spellbound, the youths wondered if the ancient magic from the story was flowing from the old man's hands into the emerging bow.

Several high pitched fawn bleats passed from Chu-no-wa-yahi's pressed lips, as he recounted how Yano-ni-yahi lured the snow white doe into bow range by imitating a distressed fawn. As the old man worked, the growling rasps of sandstone against juniper intensified the description of Yano-ni-yahi's pounding heart and the final gasps of the great white deer. As the old bow crafter finally reached the legend's climax, the boys were amazed to see that he had transformed the rough juniper stave into the fine outline of a young bow.

The old bowmaker saw in their eyes that the boys were anxious to become men and receive their tribal bows, but two acorn harvests would pass before they could enter the men's lodge and become young warriors. Chu-no-wa-yahi tried to quiet their restless spirits by telling them that the staves they had helped gather would be ready to become bows when they became men.

Earlier that spring, the boys had helped the old bowmaker gather straight juniper staves from the shadowed slopes of Waganupa, the great mountain two days north of the village. Chu-no-wa-yahi slowly wandered through the stands of juniper, carefully selecting the straightest and strongest branches. Usually, these were lower branches which grew slowly from lack of sunlight. After spying a perfect branch, he would have the agile youths carefully whittle off the stave.

Their young arms knotted in pain during the endless job of gently whittling free the tough branch. Although they were tempted to hack at the stubborn wood with the flint axe, they knew it was strictly forbidden by the old bow crafter. Hacking at the branch or attempting to break it could cause hidden lengthwise cracks that would make the stave useless. The boys learned that prized staves were to be treated with the same gentleness as a newborn.

Finally, the boys hauled the gathered staves back to the village near the base of the great cliff. There they carefully helped split and bundle them together with straight pieces of seasoned wood to keep them straight during aging. With the sapwood facing down, the staves were laid on wooden racks deep in a crevice at the base of the cliff. Protected from rain and sun, the winds of many seasons would slowly age the staves until it was their time to become bows.

The old bowmaker knew when a piece of juniper was ready to be crafted into a bow. He carefully inspected a prospective stave, first with searching eyes, and then with his calloused, tactile hands. He flexed it between his powerfully outstretched arms, and tested the sapwood with his thumbnail. Finally, he smelled the split portion of the juniper, searching for the telltale aroma of a ripely seasoned piece. Chu-no-wa-yahi told the boys how a piece of juniper, ready to be born into a bow, whispers softly to the eyes, nose, and hands: "I am strong. I am worthy. I am ready."

After the staves were cut and seasoned, the boys could not touch them. Custom strictly forbade children and women from touching man-nee. If by some careless act the bow was touched by a woman or child, it was taken to the river and washed thoroughly in sand and water. This cleansing from the earth removed any bad luck cast on man-nee by forbidden hands.

Using small flint and obsidian scraping tools and pieces of sandstone, Chu-no-wa-yahi fashioned the rough staves. He never wasted a movement. His withered hands glided gracefully back and forth like winging cliff swallows as he shaped the emerging bow. He preferred crafting during the mornings when the sun reflected off the great cliff and illuminated the wood, revealing the fine grain within.

Once a flatbow was rough shaped, the old warrior trimmed both ends until the bow spanned from his outstretched hand to his opposite hip. Using a small piece of rounded sandstone, he gently smoothed all surfaces until they flowed together in one harmonious contour. The old crafter taught the boys that the power and smoothness within man-nee depended on the perfect blending of the flat limbs into the rounded, narrower ends, and the thicker handle.

During the final sanding, Chu-no-wa-yahi would string a bow with a long sinew cord and gently draw back the string with his hand while holding the center of the bow with his outstretched foot. By raising his leg, his skilled eye could easily survey the bending arc of man-nee to ensure the balance and symmetry of both limbs. He taught the boys that the limbs must be shaped to bend in a perfect arc and in harmony, like the sweeping wings of the great eagle in flight.

After sanding was complete, the bowmaker would lean near the glowing embers of the fire and scrape away smoldering coals from two large rocks near the edge of the pit. Squinting from the hot smoke, his ancient face sometimes looked more frightening than the crazy hag. After the embers were cleared, the old man wedged one end of the bow between the closely spaced rocks and began gently bending the tip until it weakened from the heat. Once the tip was bent into a slight recurve, it was held in place between two cool rocks in the shade of the wood pile. When both ends were bent and set, the tips were slightly trimmed on the edges to accept the deer sinew bowstring.

Once man-nee was shaped into its final form, it was time for both bow and crafter to rest. Chu-no-wa-yahi would gently lay the emerging bow flat on the grass mat near the back of his crowded hut. There, the bow rested, face upward, for a full day before the tedious work of backing the new weapon began. He told the boys that man-nee, like the newborn fawn, must rest after the first day of creation.

The old man often employed the energies of the boys to chew dried sinew from deer leg tendons into a soft workable form. While they sat near the fire with puffed mouths full of fibrous sinew, the old bow crafter would prepare a fresh pot of salmon skin glue. The pungent aroma from the bubbling mixture and the constant chewing of dried deer tendons quieted both the appetite and the conversation of the boys squatted near the fire.

Before summoning the boys to his fireside, the old man would send Uni-na, the crazy one, down river for the day to collect fresh willow bark for wrapping the bow. Although she had been his woman since their youth, he could not have her near his fire when he needed unworn teeth and tireless jaws to help prepare the sinew. Even with his reassurance, her fits would have sent the boys running.

Once chewed, the sinew was separated into soft fibers, and soaked in a diluted mixture of salmon glue while the old man roughened the bow back with a coarse piece of sandstone. Chu-no-wa-yahi would then apply overlapping layers of the sticky sinew along the back of the bow. His glue-covered hands looked like two squat spiders spinning the sticky strands of sinew up and down the bow. After gluing several layers of sinew, he tightly wrapped the bow in fresh willow bark.

Protected in the back of Chu-no-wa-yahi's hut, the new bow rested for several weeks while the sinew and glue mixture cured. When it was dried, the bowmaker removed the willow bark and sanded the ragged edges of the sinew with a small piece of red sandstone. He would then hand-rub more hot salmon glue over the entire bow until it shined smooth like a snake. Finally, he wrapped a buckskin thong around the handle section. Chu-no-wa-yahi fashioned the leather grip with great care to exactly fit the hand of the new owner, allowing the bow and the hunter to function as one.

As a young man, Chu-no-wa-yahi had been praised as one of the most skillful hunters of the village. While hunting, his bow was a part of him, an extension of his spirit. His shots at running deer and flying fowl were already woven into the village's fireside stories. Over the years, his great love and respect for the bow had grown into a fascination for crafting the finest in the land. And now, every hunter in the village owned and treasured one of Chu-no-wa-yahi's magical creations. Although other men in the village made adequate bows, none matched the beauty or performance of those that emerged from the fireside of Chu-no-wa-yahi. In the hands of a patient hunter, his bows seldom failed to bring home needed game for the village. They were truly magic.

The old man's skill at crafting bows was also respected by tribes in the far hills to the east and north. Although others from different villages had tried to make bows similar to Chu-no-wa-yahi's, they failed to achieve the mystical performance of the old crafter's bows. They somehow lacked the special combination of knowledge, skill, patience, and the great love for bows that Chu-no-wa-yahi held in his heart. To the old man, creating a bow was not a labor; it was his spirit, his existence.

The two boys yearned to create bows like Chu-no-wa-yahi and

spent hours watching as he passed on his sacred craft to them. They, in turn, brightened his heart with their youthful, sparkling faces at his fireside.

The days passed without the disturbing fire-side talk of Saltu, the hated white men who were beginning to invade the lowlands to the west. Like a dark cloud over his heart, the old man feared that soon the dreaded white men would come into the hills and force the tribe back into the harsh canyons that only the deer and the eagle called home.

Nonetheless, his days with the boys were peaceful. They reminded him of his youth, and at night he dreamt of hunting deer when he was young, and in his sleep, his arms drew the imaginary bow intertwined with his spirit.

After leaving Chu-no-wa-yahi each evening, the two boys walked up the trail back to the village, renewing their vow to perfect the sacred crafting of man-nee from Chu-no-wa-yahi and someday pass it on to their sons.

During the peaceful days of clover blossom, the boys lingered near the fireside of Chu-no-wa-yahi at the base of the great cliff. But with each passing moon the old bowmaker saw the boys grow too quickly into young men, their visits becoming less frequent.

Before the annual acorn harvest, the day finally came when the boys were ceremoniously presented with their tribal bows. Manhood was theirs. The sleek bows were immaculate, the ultimate reflection of the old warrior's bowmaking skills blended with his deep love for the boys. He knew their days would now be spent on the trail of the hunter and warrior. He also knew his fireside would be hushed with a gnawing worry for their safety. A recent hunting party venturing into the lowlands near the dreaded white men had not returned. Although none would speak of it, most knew they had probably been slaughtered by Saltu and his fire-spitting sticks that thundered of death.

In the chill of a leafless night, Chu-no-wa-yahi wrestled with a terrible dream. Clutching his bow tightly in fretful sleep, he shuddered and embarked on his final journey to the land of shadows where he would hunt forever with thousands of silenced warriors before him.

Chu-no-wa-yahi escaped the anguished suffering his people would endure. In the years that followed, the raw wind howled a deathly moan at the base of the great cliff. It was joined by the mournful cries of the ever growing number of Yana killed by the invading whites.

Armed with pistols, rifles, and a vengeful hate for the strong-spirited Indians, the white men purposefully massacred the Yana, reducing the once-proud race from several thousands to less than a dozen. Battered, hunted, and clinging to life, the remnants retreated into the desolate canyons of Deer and Mill Creeks. There, under the cover of shadowed cliffs and dense brush, the survivors slipped into a secretive existence, disappearing from the white man's conquered world.

People mostly forgot about the staunch Indians known as the Yahi. But in 1908 a survey party surprised three of the primitives near Deer Creek. After shooting warning arrows at the party, two Indians abandoned an old, crippled woman and disappeared into the brush. The survey party approached the trembling woman, her withered legs wrapped in willow bark. Nearby they discovered two brush huts hidden in the dense foliage. In typical white man fashion, they ransacked the huts, confiscating bows, arrows, and primitive utensils, then left. They returned the next day hoping to find the Indians, but the huts were abandoned. The primitives had disappeared forever — except for one.

For nearly three years tales of the wild Indians of Deer Creek lingered. They were only tales — until one morning a half-starved, naked Indian was discovered in the small town of Oroville, over thirty miles from Deer Creek. Brought to bay in a corral by a barking dog, the wild Indian was captured and locked in the local jail for safekeeping. Hearing of the Indian's capture, Professor T.T. Waterman, from the Department of Anthropology at the University of California, visited the jail and established broken communication with the primitive. The Indian was Ishi, lone survivor of the Yana Indians.

Waterman befriended the fearful Indian and took Ishi to San Francisco and to the Museum of Anthropology where he became a subject of study. During his years at the museum, Ishi had little immunity to the white man's infectious world and was often sick. He was treated by Dr. Saxton Pope, instructor of surgery at the University Medical school.

Pope became friends with Ishi and admired him for his kindness, honesty, and high moral standards. And in turn, Ishi admired Pope for his ability to learn the Yana tongue and for his deep interest in Ishi's most prized possessions — his bow and arrows.

Vanquishing the barriers of culture and bonded by their common affection for the bow, Ishi and Pope grew to love each other as brothers. Ishi taught Pope how to make, shoot, and hunt Indian style, with bows and arrows. The friends spent many outings together, bows in hand, sharing a fragment of Ishi's lost world. Ishi showed Pope how to call game and how to understand the language of the birds and animals. He taught Pope how to still-hunt for deer, showing him how to use the forest sounds, the wind, and the rising sun to the hunter's advantage. And when their arrows missed game, Ishi would tell Pope the shot could easily have been made by his hero with the bow, Chu-no-wa-yahi, the great hunter and bow maker.

After three years in civilization, Pope and company returned with Ishi to his homeland along Deer Creek. It was a brief and flickering bright spot in a life that had been filled with so much terror and loneliness. Pope wrote: "We swam the streams together, hunted deer and small game, and at night sat under the stars by the camp fire, where in a simple way we talked of old heroes, the worlds above us, and his theories of the life to come in the land of plenty, where the bounding deer and the mighty bear met the hunter with his strong bow and swift arrows."

Pope planned a return trip in the fall when he and Ishi could devote more time to hunting deer with their bows and arrows. But circumstance would cheat these brothers of the bow from their autumn hunt.

Ishi fell into ill health and later contracted tuberculosis. He wilted before Pope's eyes like a wild flower plucked by the roots. In the spring of 1916 as the hills along Deer Creek once again bloomed with clover and the creek thundered with the splashes of mighty salmon, Ishi faded from the white man's world with Pope by his side.

With acorn meal, dried venison, and his treasured bow and arrows by his side, Ishi was sent on his final long journey to the land of shadows. Pope wrote: "His soul was that of a child, his mind that of a philosopher. With him there was no word for good-by. He said: 'You stay, I go.' He has gone, and he hunts with his people. We stay, and he has left us the heritage of the bow."

From the land of shadows at the base of a great cliff, huddled near a smoldering fire, to the yet unnamed bowmakers of the future; the spirit of the bow and the singing arrow lives on.

THE WINDOW

"Where is he?" muttered Ben, peering out the window into the growing darkness. He strained his neck to glimpse past the orchard and down the lane toward the back forty. "Why isn't he back yet?"

He pressed his face nearer the window, cupping a hand over his eyes to cut the reflection. Outside, the drizzle and wind had increased. Ben shivered. His eyes drifted toward the swaying branches of the apple trees, most of the leaves stripped by frost, a few apples still dangling like shiny Christmas ornaments.

His gaze melted into a blank stare. He sighed. For a moment he saw himself walking among the shadows of the trees, his recurve tucked under his arm, head bent into the drizzle, black hair shining, strong shoulders hunched against the wind. His image walked with power and purpose. Probably taking up the trail of another arrowed buck before the darn drizzle washed it out.

Ben drew back from the window and the image faded. His eyes focused on the reflection staring back. His shoulders slumped. His features sagged as if wax too close to flame. He reached up and ran fingers through white hair. He trailed his hand down parchment skin wrinkled across his cheek. Where had the black hair gone? When did all these wrinkles get here? He shook his head. Must be like watching corn grow; you never really see it sprout an inch, even if you watched it all day. But there it is by midsummer, taller than your head and tasseled before you know it. Wrinkles and white hair must be the same. Wouldn't mind getting old on the outside if my insides still didn't yearn to be young so much — like now. God, I wished I was out there with him again.

The smell of baking apples made Ben turn toward the oven. He checked his watch. How long has it been? Darn it, man, you are getting old. Can't even remember when you put the pie in. Don't let it burn for heaven's sake. Davey deserves better than burnt pie.

He rushed to the oven, put on the cooking mitts, and pulled out the pie. Whew, just browned around the edges and bubbling out the top. Perfect. You lucky old fart, you could have burned it. He set the pie on the counter. He hovered over it for a moment. The faint aroma of cinnamon wafted through the pungent odor of cooked apples. He smiled and nodded. Not half bad. Dorothy would have been proud.

Ben's brow crumpled. Dorothy, my sweet Dorothy. He reached up and pinched the bridge of his nose. Has it been two years? God, it seems like yesterday, seems like a lifetime ago. He pinched harder.

After a moment, Ben wiped his eyes and turned back toward the window. He blinked as the wetness clinging to his eyelashes blurred with the drizzle smearing the outside of the pane. A faint smile touched the corner of his mouth. If not for you, Dorothy, I wouldn't be waiting for him now. He nodded. Yep, what I couldn't give you, you gave to me. Looking out the window into the last tendrils of evening, Ben could still hear the reason in her words.

"Why turn in that boy for trespassing," she had said, "when all he really needs is someone to show him right from wrong?"

"The law and a fine will show him right from wrong, by God," Ben had said. "I sure as hell ain't no social worker for some punk who doesn't respect other folk's property."

That day Ben had worked himself into one of his steaming fits as Dorothy called them, and rightly so. He had been in his favorite stand before daylight and here came the big 10-point he'd been hunting since opening day. But suddenly the buck stiffened forty yards out, turned, and snuck off into the brush like a scolded cat. Seconds later Davey McAllister came sneaking along, toting a new bow.

Ben knew of the boy, one of the mongrels who lived down the road a mile in the trailer with their mother and a number of men who came and went, maybe a father among them. Melon thieves; mailbox vandals; trespassers; mongrels from trailers; all the same to Ben. They needed to be turned over to the law, weeded out from good folk like foxtail from between corn rows.

Ben had bailed out of the tree hotter than a hornet's behind and grabbed the boy by the collar before the kid realized what had happened. Ben had led him to the house that morning and made him sit on the porch steps. The fourteen-year-old had sat there, arms crossed, face cross, waiting for mean Ben Calaway to give back his bow after he called the law.

But Dorothy had intervened that morning, placed her hand over the phone when Ben tried to dial the sheriff and convinced him that there was a better way to handle things. Maybe she was right. Despite their love and years together, he had never been able to give her children and didn't have much understanding or tolerance of kids, especially mongrels.

"Okay," Ben had said to the boy, his voice as rough as hickory bark. "The wife thinks if I keep your bow until you rake the apples under those trees, you'll start to understand you can't go trapesin' on other folk's property. It's that or I do it my way and send you home with the sheriff."

The boy didn't say a word. A fire rose from his cheeks to become a glare in his eyes. Ben wasn't sure if he saw the boy start to cry as the kid whirled and ran off without a word. Ben had stood there shaking his head, doubting if he would ever see Davey McAllister again.

The next day when Ben stepped outside to shoot a few arrows before tending to the fields he was surprised to see Davey in the corner of the orchard raking apples. From the piles of raked apples, the kid must have been there since sunup. Ben walked past him without a word, barely nodding when the boy looked up. More fire rose into Davey's face and he said nothing. He just raked and watched Ben practice his bow, sneaking looks when he thought Ben didn't notice.

Ben snuck looks at Davey too. He saw a boy mad at life, raking with vigor to get back the one thing that meant anything to him. After a while Ben walked over and handed Davey back his bow.

"Here," he said, his face and voice softer now. "Looks like you raked enough apples. Hope you learned something."

The boy took the bow but continued to look at the apples piled near his feet. "Learned you got a lot of apples under these trees and a nice wife," Davey had said. He paused. "But what I'd really like to learn is to shoot a bow like you." The boy finally lifted his eyes to Ben.

Ben ran his fingers through his hair and looked at the boy. Awh, hell, maybe the mongrel... uh, the boy, deserved a chance. Probably never had a real dad to teach him how to shoot anyhow. Surely didn't have one who taught him how to respect the property rights of others. Ben finally nodded and led the boy to the bales. They shot. They talked some. Before Davey left that day, he thanked Ben for the lesson in shooting and for giving his bow back.

"And would you mind if I take home some of these frosted apples?" Davey had asked. "Looks like the worms and rot will get most of them. My mom don't buy none for pies. And, well," the boy flashed a shy smile, "I just go crazy for apple pie."

Of course Ben gave him apples. Davey came back and finished raking the next day after school without being asked.

"Just look at him," Dorothy had said looking out the window, "raking those apples like they were silver dollars. He's not such a bad boy. Why don't you take him hunting, Ben?"

Ben glanced out the window. "I'm not wasting my time taking some mongrel kid hunting. Certainly not on our farm, not my spot. Hell, I don't even let my brothers hunt here."

She had lifted his rigid chin in her hands.

"Listen, Ben. You've been saving your sacred deer hunting spot from others like it was a pot of gold. I don't claim to understand everything about you or your hunting, but I know you wanted to pass it on to a son — that maybe you were saving it for —"

She pressed her face in front of his. "Now look at me. It ain't happened yet and it probably ain't going to. No blame, just fact. We both know that by now. So why don't you at least pass it on to someone who would appreciate it." She had nodded toward the window.

Ben looked out that same window now, shaking his head. Hardly seems like twenty-eight years ago that Davey was out there raking apples. God, I loved that woman, even when she told me what I didn't want to hear. And of course she was right; taking that kid hunting turned out to be one of the few things I've done right with this old farm, my life. He sighed and pulled back from the window. More wind but less drizzle now. Maybe Davey will get a shot this evening after all. And who knows, maybe he'll ask me to help track. Seems like yesterday he was begging me to help track his first one. Button bucks make mighty fine first trophies. Thought the boy was going to wet his pants. God, he was excited. Funny how that excitement spreads. Even had my hands shaking trying to hold the lantern still. Guess I got to relive all the best years again through Davey. I wonder if Dorothy knew that would happen? Did you know that, Dorothy?

Ben stared at the ceiling for a moment then looked at the clock. Funny how time flies past when you think about the past, yet drags on when you wonder about the future. And when you're living for the moment, well, time just stands still somehow — like that November weekend when Davey returned from college and we both tagged identical 8-points in the back forty. Ben placed his hands on his hips. Now that was a morning to remember. I'm not sure who was prouder that day? Was that the first time Davey ever hugged me?

Ben walked over to the sink and filled the kettle with water and put it on the stove to boil. Davey will want some coffee with his pie.

Ben winced at the weight of the kettle in his grip. He flexed his fingers, the arthritic knuckles stiff and swollen. He could almost hear the gnarled joints creak like rusted hinges as he went through the motions of drawing and shooting. No more for me. He shrugged his shoulders. What the hell, tonight Davey will shoot for both of us.

Of course Dorothy knew Davey was shooting for both of us for some time. Couldn't hide a darned thing from that woman. Suppose she knew for years before she— God, she had spoiled the kid like he was her own, baking apple pies and making such a fuss every time he got a deer. Maybe that spoiling worked both ways. Having Davey around so much maybe made her hang on longer than she would have without him. Yep, he was like a son to her. Ben pinched his nose again and walked to the back door. He flicked on the porch light.

Behind him the kettle started to whistle. He pulled himself from the window and turned down the burner. He rushed back to his lookout. Any time now. My shooting gone, my Dorothy gone, my time almost gone, and now an empty window filling my life. He scratched his chin. Empty, hell, it's about to be full of something: a story, a shot, a buck, a tracking job, a hug, memories, the future. This window's got more to offer than dredging around in the past. At least it makes time almost grind to a stop.

Ben strained his neck to glimpse past the orchard and down the lane toward the back forty. Davey should be coming now. Hell, it's too dark to shoot safely. Hadn't that boy learned anything over the years? He pressed his face nearer the window, cupping a hand over his eyes to cut the reflection. He looked toward the swaying branches of the apple trees. His gaze melted into a blank stare....

For a moment, he again thought he saw himself walking among the shadows of the trees, his recurve tucked under his arm, head bent into the drizzle, black hair shining, strong shoulders hunched against the wind. The image walked with power and purpose. Probably rushing back to the house to share the news of an arrowed buck and to get the lantern to take up the trail before the darn drizzle washed it out. The image waved and held a thumbs-up, and Ben realized it wasn't his image at all but the figure of Sheriff David McAllister, a man who knew plenty about safety, a boy who had grown to respect other folk's property, liked raking apples, learned to love a gruff father he had never had, and allowed himself to be a bowhunter's son.

PQ'S NET MAN

She looked so innocent, what harm could there be in it? Heck, she was just a woman, cheated all her life out of a joy reserved mostly for outdoorsmen such as myself. She'd never tasted the sweetness of fishing.

Oh sure, she'd probably dunked a bobber off the end of a cane pole when she was a kid. But she'd never known the genuine tug of a bass stripping line off a fine reel, the silvery leap of a trout in midstream, or an unknown pull from the depths of the sea. Surely she'd never imagined the thrill and finesse of it all.

So as I sat there that spring day, picturing my new bride with rod in hand, wearing that angelic blend of naivete and innocence, I decided her time had come. I'd bless her with a rare station in life few women achieve. I'd make her a real fisherman.

I knew it wouldn't be easy. A lifetime of girlish stuff had no doubt made her all left thumbs when it came to the art of angling. And the reams of fishing savvy I'd learned over the years would be tough for her to fathom. I'd earned a modest distinction among local angling circles as a master of finny pursuits. If anyone could teach her, I could.

Our first lesson began on the rocky coast of Maine, a sea breeze brushing our faces, a clear sky reflecting off the swells. Nearby, a postcard-perfect lighthouse cast a long shadow on the incoming tide as I baited her spinner with a clam and cast her line seaward.

Fishermen along the coast say that when the tide turns inland the table is set, and it didn't take long to prove them right. I soon fell into a pattern of baiting lines and unhooking fish while my wife squealed as the stringer grew heavy with pollock, an abundant but not-too-smart shore fish. When the clam dust finally settled, we left with a cooler full of pan-sized pollock and I appropriately dubbed my bride "PQ", the Pollock Queen.

The first lesson went perfect; instill confidence in the frail ego of the beginner by letting them catch fish, lots of fish.

Now it was time to move on to lesson number two; make them appreciate the occasional full creel by showing them that fish don't always bite where and when you want.

The following weekend we planned a camping trip to northern Vermont and I was surprised when I saw PQ packing her pollock rod.

Isn't that cute, I thought. She's really fired up about this fishing thing. At least she gets an "A" for enthusiasm, but it's time to start enlightening her about the finesse of the sport. Ocean rods don't catch brookies. I draped a consoling arm across her shoulder.

"Unless you've discovered a secret inlet from the sea, I don't believe pollock inhabit Vermont waters. Maybe it's best if you leave your pollock gear home. Why don't you just enjoy the weekend camping."

"No way," she said, pulling back. "I saw you pack your fishing stuff and I'm not about to miss out on the fun. What's the matter, can't you stand a little friendly competition?"

Oh boy. I somehow couldn't muster the explanation that my gear was trout fishing paraphernalia, clearly more refined than her common sea-wetting pollock tackle. And from the set in her jaw, I didn't dare mention how trout fishing takes years of dedication and angling refinement, something a woman wasn't likely to attain, certainly not overnight. Lesson two wasn't going to be pretty.

"Sure," I said, patting her on the back. "Go ahead, take your tackle. What can it hurt?"

Besides, I knew my 5 A.M. departure the next morning would find her still curled in the bottom of her sleeping bag dreaming of a leisurely 10 o'clock breakfast of quiche at some country inn.

She must have been hungry early that morning. I no sooner stepped from the tent under the pale glow of first light when a raspy "HEY" bellowed from the depths of her sleeping bag.

"Where do you think you're going? You're not try to sneak off without me, are you?"

"Who? Me? Why no," I lied. "I was going to get the boat ready down by the lake. Make sure your cushion was dry and everything."

Moments later, she stumbled out the tent door, rubbing an eye with one hand, the other hand clutching her pollock rod. Okay, so I was wrong. The shy trout will soon cure her blind enthusiasm. Lesson number two coming up — it ain't always easy.

As I rowed across the mirrored lake toward a likely looking point of rocks, she dipped an oversized worm into the water. She had stuck the thing on a number 4 nickel hook clipped directly to her pollock snap swivel. Never, not a trout. In the early light her face wore confidence underscored with determination. Poor girl. Her simpleton attempts might snag a perch at best. Oh well, like Dad always said, experience is the best teacher.

I had just tied a delicate spinner on my ultra-light when she screeched, "I think I have a trout!"

Wishful thinking. I knew better. But as I turned to watch her folly, PQ hoisted a fat rainbow from the water. No, this isn't happening. Check it, maybe it's blind? I sat there shaking my head.

"Don't sit there like a dummy. Hurry, grab him," she said, swinging the fish in my direction.

PQ landed the trout neatly in my lap where it immediately flopped off the hook and slithered down my hip-boot. I lurched backward kicking frantically trying to oust the wriggling thing from my sock. PQ turned into comedian and outdoor photographer as she began snapping pictures and laughing hysterically. Fisherman in the other boats around the lake looked and pointed in our direction. Great. I put on my sunglasses and pulled down the brim of my hat. I'd deal with the film later.

By the time I rowed back to camp to change my slimy pants, she had caught three more of the worm-gluttonous trout. They obviously didn't possess enough refinement to chase my trouty lures. Probably hatchery fish that didn't know any better.

At the dock PQ hoisted her catch and hollered loud enough for half of Vermont to hear, "See, being a trout fisherman isn't such a BIG deal."

The sounds of laughing gulls echoed across the lake. I looked skyward. None soared, but boats in the distance rocked.

It was 10 o'clock when PQ finished eating her fried trout breakfast.

"Those tasted fabulous," she said rubbing her sides and stretching. "Better than the country inn any day. Sure you don't want some? I'll be glad to share."

"No thanks. My coffee here is just fine. I'm not partial to lake-caught rainbows anyway."

They probably tasted a tad wormy, certainly bitter.

I gladly broke camp after we agreed to head north and enjoy the scenery along Vermont's back roads. Besides, I'd had my weekend's fill of fishing and grinned as I watched the lake disappear in the rearview mirror. I ignored the other campers and fishermen waving good-bye. PQ hung out the window and waved back. "Save a few big ones for me," she hollered.

We'd driven less than an hour when PQ grew tired of the scenery. She turned to me with that same look she had on her face back at the lake.

"Hey, fishin' partner, I've got a great idea."

I was afraid to ask. I swallowed.

"Why don't we stop somewhere and catch a whole mess of those trout so we can have big fish fry? We'll invite my mother and everything. You know how she loves fresh fish. What do you say?"

What could I say? She was no doubt recalling her cooler of pollock and somehow had crossed the idea with her odd stroke of luck that morning on the lake. The two events had now sparked the misconception that trout everywhere must be easy prey for any neophyte who happened by. Linear thought, dangerous. It must be a female thing. I was about to explain how quality trout waters just don't set along Vermont highways like road-side picnic tables when she demanded, "Pull over! Let's try our luck right there in that cute little pond."

There, next to the road, sat a cattail-lined marsh where years ago someone had scooped out a few of loads of gravel. Little it was. Cute it wasn't. I looked at her in disbelief and shook my head. A chub couldn't live in that muck pit let alone a sporting fish like a trout.

"Come on," she said, poking me in the shoulder. "Don't be such a stick-in-the-mud. Can't you tell a hot spot when you see it?"

One of us obviously couldn't. What was the sense in arguing? Let the hand of hard knocks teach her. I pulled off the blacktop and sat there smugly looking at the water, its matting of duckweed clearly proclaiming no trout lived there. Hopeless, utterly hopeless.

"Better get with it, mister," PQ said, as she hopped from the car and grabbed her rod. "By the time you're ready, I'll have 'em flippin' on the shore."

She bounded down the bank to the edge of the pond, startling a bull frog that plopped into the murk. I hid my grin. Where frogs live, trout don't. It's a fact of fishing. Plain and simple. It should have been lesson number three.

"Gee, that's a pretty small pond," I said with an innocent sigh. I folded my arms and sat back. "I wouldn't want to ruin all your fun by catching the only fish in there. Go ahead, you knock 'em dead."

Unblinking, she tied on one of her rusted pollock lures and cast it into the lone circle of water free of duckweed. As it hit, the water swirled and a bronze flash boiled the surface. No, it couldn't be. My throat tightened as a hefty brook trout jumped from the pool with PQ's lure jammed in its mouth.

Stunned, I stumbled from the car and slid down the bank with landing net in hand. I reached for the water's edge but oozy muck grabbed at my new sneakers and I back-peddled. At least I tried. Crazed by the frenzied tug on her rod, PQ shoved me forward, screaming, "Quick, net my fish before he gets off!"

The steep bank and slippery muck did the rest. The next thing I knew I was sitting in a foot of water with a brookie thrashing between my legs. As instructed, I netted PQ's trout.

By the time I found the stringer and shed my mucky clothes, PQ had four more brookies flipping on the bank. Like the pollock and rainbows, she caught the brookies almost as fast as I unhooked and put them on the stringer. When the action finally ended, I sat staring blankly at the ground, eating dust from passing traffic. PQ sauntered up and dangled her flopping catch in front of my nose.

"Ain't trout fishin' somethin' else?" she said, slapping me on the back.

I prayed it had to be.

For nearly a month, I searched for a logical explanation for her beginner's luck and my failure to read Vermont ponds. I tossed at night pondering the question while PQ lay beside me, her face traced with a contented smile, occasionally twitching her rod hand. Finally, I convinced myself the entire trip was merely a fluke, nothing more than a few half-starved trout, probably retarded half-breeds of chubs.

I shuddered at the thought of what fishing lesson number four might bring and soon took up a new interest; bowhunting. That autumn I even planned a bowhunting vacation to Colorado's high country. PQ agreed to go along and enjoy the camping, read some books, and take a few pictures. At least there were no pollock and probably few trout where we were headed.

Nonetheless, PQ bought a new trout rod and reel for the trip, a fancy ultra-light. She'd read in one of her new fishing magazines about some dude catching trout in Yellowstone and wanted to get in on the action, as she called it. She didn't seem the least concerned when I told her we weren't going within three hundred miles of the place. She just smiled. I rolled my eyes and packed the car.

We no sooner set up our tent near a small Colorado trail head when PQ cornered an old-timer filling a water bag at the campground pump. She'd seen him ride in on horseback and rushed over to get the local scoop. I sauntered over too.

“Is there anyplace to catch a trout around here, mister?” she asked.

He cocked his head then scratched his stubble while sizing her up.

“Well, you see, we're really bowhunting,” I said, palms up. “Seen any mulies?”

PQ flashed me a look as sharp as a laser-honed hook. The old timer paid me little attention.

“Why you askin', missy? You some kinda trout fisherman?”

“You better believe it.” she said, throwing back her shoulders. “Can't wait to set my hook into a Rocky Mountain trout. I hear they're mighty fine in the pan.”

Set my hook into? Mighty fine in the pan? Where'd she get those lines? I bit my lip. The old-timer grinned.

“Well, missy,” he said, pushing back his tattered hat, “down in that thicket yonder thar's a crick that the range cattle drink out of. You drove through it gettin' in here. It ain't much to look at but there's some old beaver dams downstream that hold a few cutthroat. Late mornin's the best time to try. That's about the only fishin' 'round these parts.”

PQ nodded hopefully and pumped the old guy's hand. His grin broadened into a toothless smile. She wheeled and trotted back to the car, pulling out her new rod.

The old timer leaned toward me.

“Looks like you got a handful there, partner, a real fishin' fool.”

I nodded. If he only knew.

“About those deer,” he continued. “Mulies everywhere, son. You shouldn't have any problem gettin' one. Even beginners get ‘em up here.”

I thanked him then hurried back to the car. I yanked out my take-down recurve and began putting it together. That evening I hunted without much luck. Early the next morning too. I headed back to camp around 10 and decided to spend some time relaxing with PQ who had kept herself occupied reading paperbacks — mysteries mostly, not an angling book in the lot.

The late morning sunshine revealed a glow in her cheeks and I was thinking romance when she smiled at me and nodded toward the tent. I nodded back. Why not? She sprang to life. In a flash she unveiled her rod and reel and donned her new fishing hat. She'd been nodding toward the creek.

"I bet we catch some fat ones for dinner," she said handing me the net.

"Gee, I'd love to go with you, but I forgot to bring my gear. Sorry, I guess I'll have to sit this one out."

Then, spreading one of her sly grins, PQ sauntered over to the car and pulled out my trout rod.

"I knew you wouldn't want to miss the action, so I packed it for you. You can thank me later. We better hurry now before the sun gets too high."

There was no way out.

PQ pulled me along toward the brook where the cutthroats were supposed to live. The trickle barely wetted a wide bed of rocks. Two cows drinking upstream would probably dry up the little seep. Surely the old guy had been pulling her leg. No trout could live in that. It couldn't support a crawfish let alone a trout. PQ, however seemed oblivious to the lack of water and ordered me downstream while she went upstream.

My God, she's got to know that fish need water to live in. Oh well, lesson number four coming up — no water, no fish.

I sat down in the shade of a cottonwood. No sense in wasting good nap time. Gazing into the trickle, I was a bit surprised when I spotted a minnow gasping for oxygen. I couldn't imagine how he'd got there. As I mused whether the poor little guy would perish from loneliness or suffocation, PQ yelled.

"Hey ! There's a big trout up here, and I'm gonna catch him. Get ready with that net."

I leaned back against the tree and murmured, "That's nice. Holler when you've got him."

I pulled my cap down over my eyes. Must be the effects of thin mountain air. Poor woman, probably seeing things. That, or a reflection of some fish-shaped rock was playing tricks on novice eyes. She should have bought some Polaroid glasses.

A shriek jolted me from my siesta.

"I got him, I got him. Come help me!"

I splashed upstream over the slippery rocks. Rounding the bend, I couldn't believe my eyes. There, next to a small pool stood PQ, rod thrashing wildly, a huge cutthroat straining at the end of her line.

I rushed in to land the fish. Rather than be pushed into the water, this time I just waded in and scooped out her trout. Who could have imagined? The chunky cutthroat measured over a foot and a half.

Had to weigh a good three pounds. My jaw hung almost to the water, my pride somewhere below it.

"A real beaut of a trout, huh?" PQ said, hands on hips, head cocked in triumphant. "Where's your stringer, net man? Can't waste all day eyeballin' one fish. Let's get a move on."

I could only manage a weak, "Un-un-unbelievable."

For the next hour I followed PQ upstream, netting her fish at each pool, tending her stringer, and trailing behind like a lost puppy. When the action finally ended, her stringer hung heavy with trout, paining more than my arm on the way back to camp. Inside my stomach grew a hollow ache like a gnawing animal wanting to be free. It wouldn't go away.

For the next five days I moped around the mountains, toting my bow, only half looking for mule deer. Never spotted a one. The old guy must have been pulling my leg. PQ caught all the fish either of us could eat, especially considering my loss of appetite, so we decided to cut the vacation short.

On our way home we camped one final night in Rocky Mountain National Park. After putting up the tent, I began gathering wood for an evening fire. Nothing relaxes like a campfire. And boy, did I need some relaxing.

Just as I struck the match, PQ leaned over and blew it out.

"Silly boy. You're not supposed to start the fire until AFTER we've caught dinner. What kinda camper are you?"

I wondered. Maybe Motel Six was just down the road. I was positive they didn't have trout in their pool.

"Come along now. Sun's a settin'. We don't want to miss the trout's evening feed, do we?"

My knotted stomach cried out, Yes, yes we do. Not the stream, please. Not tonight. No more fishing lessons. I give. But I hid my weakness and painted my best angling savvy face.

"I'm afraid it's too late. It'll be dark within the hour and the last good river we crossed is twenty miles back down the road. A nice thought though."

"Oh," she said with an innocent smile, "I wasn't thinking of anything that complicated. We can just fish this nice stream right here in the campground. Let's give it a try."

My eyes widened.

"You can't possibly mean this one that flows right past these hundreds of campsites. Just look at the beaten path along its banks.

It's been fished by every greenhorn in the Rockies. You can't really mean this stream."

"Sure. Why not? It looks fine to me. Come on, don't be a party-pooper."

I just shook my head and followed. It was no use explaining. Her logic didn't follow conventional fishing wisdom anyway. Lesson number five coming up; you can't catch fish where 10,000 other anglers have wetted lines all summer.

PQ lead the way down the foot path along the river as it meandered through the middle of the campground. Undaunted by the hordes who had fished before her, she followed the trail into the shallow current and began frothing the water with her short spasmodic casts, all the while wearing a blissful smile of anticipation.

We fished for a half-hour without so much as a follow. Ha, the game was finally turning my way. Now we'll see who begins to understand the art of fishing. I spotted a three-incher darting for cover. He looked lonely and scared. Big surprise. I knew it was hopeless but I wasn't about to tell her so. No, let the river exact its own punishment on the foolish.

On the next cast, PQ hooked and skidded in that poor three-incher. The pitiful thing looked half as big as her pollock spinner.

"What a dinky fish!" she whimpered, obviously aghast that a trout fisherman of her accomplishments had caught such a puny prize.

I shrugged my shoulders. "He's probably the largest trout within a mile of this place. So let's go back and roast a hot dog. Can't knock 'em dead every time."

Without a word, she released the runt and resumed casting. At long last I detected the bitterness of fishing failure on her pressed lips. Humility builds character. Good, finally, she would realize that becoming a true fisherman takes time, skill, and dedication. No more flukes, no more half-starved retarded fish, no more innocent gloating over —

"FISH ON!" she roared.

The stream exploded in a silvery spray as a trout burst from the water, PQ's spinner locked in its jaws. As humble servant and net man, I scooped up the robust brookie and groped for my stringer. A fresh pain knotted my gut while PQ cranked in another fine mess of fish in the failing light. Where had they come from? No cover, no feed, just barren looking water. By sunset it was over. Completely.

As we stepped from the stream, a throng of campers, no doubt roused by PQ's shouting, crowded around us.

"Man, look at those brookies!"

"What a super catch!"

"How'd ya hook 'em?"

Taking on the role of the old pro I'd once been, PQ wore the modest, almost smug face of a seasoned angler. She lingered for effect. The crowd oohed and aahed. From the back, an older gent wearing a worn fishing vest dangling with lures pushed his way forward.

"I'll be damned," he said thumbing his jaw. "Who'd of ever thought trout like those lived here in water like that. You two must be fishin' fools."

I nodded toward PQ. "It was the ol' fishin' wizard here who slayed 'em again."

PQ lifted her chin. A twinkle flashed in her eyes as the seasoned angler gave her that look of admiration shared among fishermen. Even in the pale light the glow in her cheeks shined clearly. She turned and headed for camp.

The old gent's eyes drifted over to me and lingered for a second before lowering to his feet. He scuffed at the ground. Why had he looked away from my face? Did he somehow know I was a broken man?

He winced as an elk bugled off in the distance. Its musical trumpet echoed through the valley. I perked up and turned an ear toward the sound.

"You must be an elk hunter," he said. "I can see that look in your eye."

The tension eased, I smiled. "Yeah, sorta, just started bowhunting this season. Already feel like I want to do it the rest of my life."

"I know what you mean," he offered, stepping closer. "I used to think there was nothing like it. Bowhunted for thirty years. But I finally gave it up for fishing."

I looked into his eyes. He too wore circles. I seemed to recognize that haunted expression. Or was it just his age?

"Elmer!" a woman hollered, from the shadows. "Come on you old pack horse, get your backside movin'. Can't you hear them elk? Man, we gotta break camp and get to our huntin' grounds before sunup."

Elmer's shoulder's bunched around his neck like a turtle taking cover. "Yes dear," he said, turning away. "Coming soon, just visiting here."

A husky woman wearing a camo jacket strode up to him and wrapped a bearlike arm around him.

"Did you hear that? Wow, Elmer, they ought to be going crazy tomorrow. Maybe you can show me how to call one in? I been practicing. I'll shoot him, you pack him — just like we did that buck last week. Come on, hon, let's hurry."

He turned and waved, the evening shadows stealing the last of his sickly smile. Their shadows disappeared down the trail.

"Do you think we're gettin' too old to try for a moose, Elmer? I was reading about it in my bowhunting magazine and got to thinking about next year."

Even in the distance, Elmer's sigh sounded like the air escaping from a punctured inner tube.

I shook my head and turned after PQ's silhouette far down the trail. Another elk sounded in the distance. I pictured poor Elmer hunched under the weight of an elk quarter lashed to a pack frame.

Suddenly, netting a few fish didn't seem so bad. I grabbed my net and rushed after PQ. As I caught up to her, she turned and wrapped an arm around my waist.

"You're one hell of a netman, mister."

I glanced down at the reflection of the fish on the stringer and my mouth started to water. Fresh brookies pan-fried over an open fire. Yeah, it could be a lot worse.

The following story is a chapter from Dan's novel, ***Opening Day*** *— the saga of a fifteen-year-old hunter struggling to discover himself among his peers while the runaway forces of nature and circumstance plunge them all into a deadly spiral of survival.*

STORY TIME

An hour after dark, Brad and Corey stumbled through the cabin door, cheeks scoured red, lips pale blue.

Brad's grandfather turned from the kitchen stove, a dripping ladle in one hand, the other propped on his hip, ermine-white eyebrows bunching at the sight of them. He shook his head and turned back to his brew.

Brad stomped crusted snow from his boots. Crap, why doesn't he ask me why we're late? At least that would gimme a chance to explain — or try to if any of them will believe me. God, I hardly believe it myself. Well, maybe with Corey backing me up they won't accuse me of telling another whopper anyway.

Brad's father and the others rushed from the cabin's living room to get a look.

"You had us awfully worried, son," Al said mildly, stepping into the kitchen. "Why don't you give me your coats so I can hang them to dry. You look half frozen. I think you should grab a bowl of Granddad's stew and come in and sit near the pot-bellied stove. After you get some hot food in you, then maybe you can explain why you were out so late."

Without a word the boys obliged. Hunched like old men, they shuffled into the living room. With steaming bowls cradled in their laps, they huddled together on a split pine bench near the stove and propped their feet on a log. Their teeth chattered. Steam rose from their pant legs. The smell of wet wool soon mixed with the aroma of venison stew.

Brad slurped from a spoon. Okay, so where do I begin? Should I first tell them about what I saw in Deadman's Swamp? Heck, I'm not even sure what I saw. It wasn't a coon, I'm sure of that. It was way too big, whatever it was — Naw, I better just stick to what Corey saw too. That's the only way they'll believe me.

He peeked up from his bowl. Warren Crane stood nearby sipping scotch and water. He too wore flushed cheeks, peppered with the purple streaks of minute blood vessels like tiny red worms working their way to the surface. But he didn't look cold. The upper half of his wool shirt gaped open and the hair that usually carefully covered most of his bald spot stood fluffed in a tousle — probably a new hairdo courtesy of his hunting hat.

Brad almost snickered between gulps. He looks more like a circus clown tiring in the third act than my dad's boss. If he doesn't watch it, he might start acting normal like a regular guy. The almighty Mr. Crane, a mere mortal? He'd probably puke at the thought.

Brad glanced toward his dad's best friend, Vern Larsen, who slumped in a nearby rocker as if halfway to a coma. Beer cans littered the small table next to him, a fresh one clasped in his hand. He seemed locked in a trance, staring at the small icing-glass plate in the stove door. A flickering reflection danced in his watery eyes like flashes of thought going nowhere. In his other hand hung a cigarette, its long ash drooping from neglect, smoke slithering up between his fingers.

Brad gulped the last of his stew, wiped the corner of his mouth with the back of his hand, and set the bowl aside. He squirmed on the bench trying to find a comfortable position. He reached down and rolled up his drying pant legs to expose the damp socks and long johns underneath. He glanced around. All the eyes in the room had settled on him, silent, waiting. Uh oh, story time. I mean, time for the truth. But now it's going to sound more like one of my stories. I could at least make a story sound real enough to be true; but how do I deal with the impossible truth? Brad fingered his lip as if searching for the right words to begin.

Before he could start, his grandfather broke the ice.

"You two must have found a buck crossing better than any I've seen in forty years to keep you out after dark," he said, the pale blue of his eyes glacial behind his glasses.

Fiddling with his cuffs, Brad started softly.

"Yeah, we found some good buck crossings alright, but none that kept us out so late. That's not what happened." Brad looked to Corey for support and found him hiding behind the rim of his tipped bowl. Great, some best friend. Where's that motor-mouth when I need it?

Al leaned against one of the upright beams near the stove, cradling a mug of coffee. “Come on, son, let’s get to the point. Why don’t you tell us what happened, exactly what happened.”

Brad glanced over at him. Geez, why can’t he yell at me like a real father? Doesn’t he care? Isn’t he pissed? I mean, crap, I could have been killed or lost or something. At least he could raise his voice. Or is he too afraid to show a little backbone in front of Crane?

Brad dug his fingers into the wool of his pants and continued.

“We found some spots with rubs along that part of ridge near the swamp where you took us, Dad. Built two stickups there too, just like Granddad showed us. And with this fresh snow it ought to be perfect there tomorrow.”

Brad’s face brightened at the prospect.

“Enough about your stickups,” Granddad said. “We want to know why you foolishly stayed out so late in this kind of weather. If you two don’t have any more sense than to stay out after dark in the middle of a snowstorm, maybe you can’t be trusted to go hunting at all. You want to be grown up enough to hunt deer in the big woods, yet you pull some childish stunt like this. What are we supposed to think?”

“I think we ought to make ‘em chop wood all day and keep camp clean,” Vern slurred, breaking his stupor long enough to fuel the fire.

Brad bolted forward. What? Stay in camp opening day? That’s not fair.

Corey sputtered a mouthful of stew back into his bowl. His cheeks puffed and eyes widened. He finally found his tongue.

“Wa-wa-wait a minute, Mr. Mercer. We can explain, honest. It wasn’t our fault. We got attacked. Had to run for our lives, well, kind of. Then we got mixed up in the snowstorm. A little lost, that’s all. No big deal.”

“Attacked?” Al said, his voice reaching tenor. “Who? Where? What happened?”

Crane and Vern scooted to the edge of their seats. Granddad canted his neck like a heron ready to strike.

“No, not that,” Brad said, “Nobody attacked us. Not a person. It was nothing like that. It was a coon, a big crazy raccoon.”

“Right,” Vern snickered and slapped his knee. “You’d better check what these punks been smoking out in the woods. Sounds like they got a bad batch making them see charging coons. What a crock.” He drowned his whinny laugh with a gulp of beer.

Brad’s jaw bunched. Damn, I knew it. I knew this would happen. Now they’ll never believe about the other thing I saw in the swamp.

"We're not burnouts," Corey said, green eyes glaring, more redness rising into already fiery cheeks. "If we were wasteoids, we wouldn't be here having a straight good time — or at least trying to."

Vern shrugged off the comment, finding refuge in another slug of suds.

"Come on, Dad. You know better than that. Corey and I got chased by this crazy raccoon. It was either sick or really mad at us. Maybe both."

"Look, son," Al said, stepping closer, his eyes softening as he knelt before Brad. "I know you like to glamorize your little adventures. That's okay sometimes, we've kind of grown to expect it. But you have to understand, this isn't the time for it. We have to know the truth."

Brad nodded. He cleared his throat and began, and without interruption, he recounted the entire episode, every detail in place. Corey nodded stiffly at each point in the story. Vern even managed to sit on the edge of his chair without butting in.

"...and by the time we finally found the trail road again, it was dark. We somehow ended up near the far end of the trail down by the swamp. It took a while to walk back in this heavy snow. Must be knee-deep out there by now. But we're all right. Nothing serious happened."

"Sounds like you kids pushed that coon too far," Crane said, snorting and scratching his belly. "Maybe you forgot whose home you were in? It doesn't surprise me that it wanted to sink its teeth into you. Not a very bright trick, I'd say. But then again, I'm not surprised." Crane turned and glanced toward Al.

Brad looked into his lap. Thanks, Mr. Crane, you're just what I needed, more gas on the fire. The way my dad follows your every lead, I'll be lucky to see my rifle again. Yeah, thanks a lot.

"All we did was run it up a tree," Corey said, holding his palms up. "It's not like we were out there trying to hurt it. Why would that have made it go bonkers?"

Brad's eyes drifted to Granddad. He propped his elbows on his knees and leaned forward.

"Coons are dang ornery," Granddad said. "And they can be mean-tempered scrappers for their size. But they don't normally go around chasing people through the woods, even if they are mighty irritated. Just ain't natural."

"If I had brats chasing me like mad dogs wielding sticks, I'd try for a chunka-their-asses-too," Vern offered, his words bunching into a slur at the end. He tossed another empty into the bag near his feet.

"Natural or not," Brad said quickly to cut off Vern's venom, "it's true, all of it. And if Corey hadn't dazed it with his stick, it might still be after us. That thing was crazy like I've never seen."

"Was it drooling or foaming around the mouth?" Al asked.

"Couldn't see," Corey said. "Had so much snow on its face it was hard to tell. All I know is that its eyes looked weird. Like it was stoned," he flashed Vern a look, "or had too many beers."

The stab went unheard as Vern clattered in the bottom of his carton for a full can.

Granddad rubbed his chin, his silver stubble making a slight hiss under his thumb. "Maybe it had rabies," he said. "Coons carry it. That would account for it wandering around in this heavy snow. Rabies, yep, it's the only thing that makes any sense."

"Rabies?" Crane said, wagging his face. "You're kidding? I thought only dogs got rabies. Come on."

"Nope," Granddad said. "Most domestic animals like dogs get rabies vaccines. They can't get it then. It's usually wild animals like bats, skunks and coons that get it; predators and omnivores. They say the virus is transmitted through the saliva of a carrier from either its bite or from eating saliva-infected carrion."

"Carrion?" Vern asked, screwing his face up and sticking his tongue out. "You mean like some kind of rotten crap along the roadside. I thought coons were clean, always washing their food first."

"Only on staged nature shows," Granddad said. "Sure, they wash scavenged food around water, but they're opportunists mostly, like miniature bears. In the wild they'll eat whatever handout comes along. And they don't much care how or where they get it — carrion included."

"Sounds to me like half the lazy-asses on welfare nowadays," Crane said, tossing down the last of his scotch. "A bunch of good-for-nothing opportunists, the whole lot of them. I guess it's no wonder they call them, 'coons'."

His jowls shook as he chuckled at his wit. No one else joined in, not even Vern. Al pushed his hands into his pockets and looked away.

Brad was pleasantly surprised by the embarrassment in his dad's eyes. Maybe Dad can't stand the fat toad any more than the rest of us? Hmmm, maybe he puts up with him because of us?

"But rabies, this far north?" Al finally asked, breaking the tension.

"Only logical answer," Granddad said. "Makes sense too. I remember seeing mad dogs when I was a kid, long before they developed rabies vaccine. Pain drove them loco. It attacks their nervous system and works into the spinal area, eventually the whole brain. Drives them crazy. They'll tear into anything in their path."

"Sounds awful," Corey said, drawing his legs up close to his chest. "If that coon got rabies around here, do you suppose other animals like wolves or coyotes could get it? Or a deer or bear? That'd be awesome!"

Granddad pushed his glasses back up the bridge of his nose and bunched his eyebrows.

"Guess it's possible," he said after a moment. "I've even heard of cows getting it after being bitten by infected foxes, but, whoa, that's really stretching things, even for a story-teller." His eyes drifted over to Brad.

Brad looked away from Granddad toward the flicker in the stove. Why do they always look at me? So I stretched a few fish when I was a kid, cried wolf now and then. Big deal. It was just for fun, I didn't know any better then. Can't they see I've changed? Heck, I'm grown up now. Can't they tell the difference?

"Never heard of a bear getting rabies," Granddad continued. "Then again, maybe nobody ever lived to tell about meeting up with one. Just to be safe we better report this coon thing to the Natural Resources people. They'll want to know about a possible outbreak of rabies. Have to wait until we can make it into town though. And no telling when that will be with this snow storm."

Vern stood from his chair, swaying a little in front of the makeshift window where a scavenger had broken in. Outside, the storm worsened. Waves of snow pushed against the plastic like a heavy hand.

"Probably a whole pack of them rabid wolves out there right now," he said, gazing in the boys' direction, as if looking for something to focus on, "just frothing at the mouth at the thought of you juicy smurfs. Yep, I'd sure hate to be you guys come morning in the swamp."

He took another long draw from his can and edged closer to the boys. "That's right," he continued, "them wolves probably realize we're the only easy food anywhere around this big old swamp. They're probably planning right now — making some horrible trap for first light when they can lay in hiding behind the outhouse, wait for you to get busy trying to find yourselves... Then sneak up behind you and... MAKE BREAKFAST OUTTA YA!" He leaped at the boys, snarling, his sour breath causing them to draw back.

Vern broke into his whinnying laugh. Crane joined him. Brad scowled. His eyes met Corey's. Corey glanced sideways at Vern, as if to say: Can you believe this guy?

"Don't try to scare us," Corey said, his green eyes flashing back at Vern. "We're not that green. A pack of wolves up here? Get real."

"I've heard that rabies can spread pretty fast through an area," Granddad said. "but it ain't likely there's a whole pack of rabid wolves running around the swamp. They'd be too sick to run in a pack. Besides, I doubt if there's enough wolves around here to make up a pack."

"But it could happen!" Vern shouted as he shook his finger at Granddad. The turn in the conversation had somehow stirred his senses to life. "If it happens to wild dogs then it can happen to wolves. Admit it, old man. Admit it!"

"On second thought," Granddad said, turning slightly and winking at the boys, "you could be right, Vern. Matter of fact, that frothing pack might decide to pick us off one at a time as we head to the outhouse in the morning. And for their sake, I hope they know which one of us is full of horsecrap!"

The room filled with laughter. Vern frowned for a moment, then, unsure of who to sneer at, slipped into laughter despite himself. Corey and Brad rocked back and forth slapping their knees. Granddad wore a smile prouder than if he'd just landed a three-pound trout.

Just as the laughing began to ebb into giggles and snorts, Brad glimpsed something flicker outside past the plastic window. A swirl of snow?

A dark shape neared the window then was gone. Brad gasped and gripped Corey's leg. Corey had seen it too. They stiffened, eyes flaring. The others saw their reaction and turned toward the window. The room fell deathly silent.

Outside the window, a low moan rose and fell. Gasps hissed inside the room like the sounds of ladies sipping tea. The moan lasted only a moment, almost blending with the snow and wind. But it was there nonetheless. Everyone heard it and held their breath. Vern dropped his beer can, its clank splitting the thin silence. Al glared at him.

The moaning rose again, this time more clearly. Vern shuffled away from the window until the heat of the stove stopped him. Crane pushed himself back on the sofa, his mouth agape, eyes fixed on the plastic.

As the moan died, a faint scratching grated the outside of the wall, like a branch swaying in the wind. But unlike a branch, the sound moved along the outside wall, inching closer to the door, like long claws searching for a way in.

"For God's sake, Mercer," Crane hissed, "do something, damn it. And do it quick."

Granddad nodded toward the gun rack. Al scurried across the floor and jerked his .30-06 Remington from the pegs. He grabbed a full clip from the rack's shelf and jammed it into the magazine. With a jerk of the hand, he pulled back the bolt, chambering a soft-nosed shell, the bolt clacking sharply in the stilled room. He leveled the rifle at his waist.

The scratching stopped.

Everyone listened.

Nothing.

"It heard you, Dad," Brad finally whispered. "Maybe you scared it away. Maybe it —"

Brad gulped air as the scratching resumed. This time it grew louder and had moved to the kitchen door leading to the shed. Claws, big claws for sure now. The boys crowded together. Granddad stood firm, head cocked. He cupped his ear and listened.

The scratching grew into a clattering at the door, then a pounding. The rusty hinges creaked and the door knob began to rattle.

"It's that goddamn bear that broke your window," Crane said, his droopy features drawn tight like he had lost fifty pounds. "It came back and now it's coming in here. Shoot the sonofabitch through the door! Shoot, Mercer, before it gets in here again."

Al shouldered his rifle and pressed his cheek against the stock. Despite Crane's orders, his finger stayed clear of the safety and trigger.

"Wait!" Granddad said, a slight smile forming, grabbing the barrel of rifle and pushing the muzzle down. "Don't shoot, I think we know this bear."

Puzzled faces turned.

The pounding stopped.

The boys let out held breaths.

But they sucked them back in as the door knob shuddered anew then began turning slowly. The boys jumped as a gust of wind ripped open the door, snow billowing into the kitchen like a ghost from the night. Vern staggered back into the stove, cursing as he singed his arm. Crane pressed himself back to the top of the sofa.

For a moment only silence and cold air engulfed the room. Then the moaning began again from the darkness of the shed.

"Yoooo, yoo, yoo hoo. Yoo-hoo, is anybody in there?"

Al sighed and almost dropped the rifle.

"Come on in you nasty ol' bear," he hollered, "before I change my mind and shoot you anyway. You're letting in the cold. Fun's over. Get your crazy butt in here."

Granddad chuckled and shook his head.

From the darkness stepped Larry Mercer, Al's younger brother. Looking like a bear, he moved though the doorway with a blend of power and grace, his bulky sloping shoulders leading the way ahead of a long torso that appeared oversized for his narrow hips and squat legs. He kicked the door shut behind him and stepped into the light of the overhead gas lamp. He yanked off a wool lumberman's hat and shook his head. Wet snow sprayed from his beard and mane of hair, both thick and shining like the prime fur of a bear rug.

"Howdy, slicks. Good to see ya."

His broad face lit up like neon, undersized chestnut eyes glistening like those of a wild creature. He reached up and yanked at the icicles hanging from his handlebar moustache.

"Holy crow, it's cold out there. If I didn't know better, I'd say it was January instead of mid-November."

He stomped snow from his full-laced logging boots, shiny slick with bear grease. He fingered the buttons on his long plaid wool jacket and laid back its oversized collar.

"Man," whispered Corey, "he looks like he stepped out of time machine. Right from an 1890's lumber camp."

Brad nodded and smiled. "Uncle Larry! You scared the pants off us."

Larry grinned and nodded toward Brad's rolled up cuffs. His eyes shined even brighter.

"Well, by God it looks like I did a little. Must be getting better at these pranks in my old age." He ended with a laugh that would have shamed Santa as he plopped down two bulky rucksacks. But he tenderly set a long deer-skin case in the corner. He turned and winked at Corey. "It's my job to scare these city slickers. Somebody's got to keep them on their toes, sharpen city-fied senses."

Larry paused, suddenly sensing the concern still fresh in everyone's face. He nodded to the cabin's regulars, Crane and Vern.

"Gee, sorry, guys. I didn't mean to scare you that much. I figured you'd know better, especially you, Dad." He strode over and wrapped a big arm around Granddad. Granddad reached up and patted him on the shoulder.

"It's just that we didn't expect you until early tomorrow morning," he said. "You caught us off guard, that's all."

Larry nodded toward the rippling plastic across the window.

"No way I could wait until morning. There's a nasty northeaster blowing in and I figured I better get back in here tonight or I wouldn't make it at all. Took me nearly two hours just to drive the 50 miles from Munising. The snow is already belly deep to a coyote in the woods. I parked my Jeep three miles down the trail near the gravel road. The snow drifted across that first hollow in the trail. Even with four-wheel drive I didn't want to risk getting stuck there so I played it safe and parked off to the side. If it snows all night at least I can walk out to my Jeep and four-wheel it back to town. No sense me being stranded here after I get my buck. Let's hope it melts some by the time you slicks try and get out with that two-wheel tank of yours."

He shook more wet snow from his jacket and hung it on a peg on one of the posts. He held his hands near the stove. He looked back at the window.

"Grouse fly through the window?"

No one answered at first.

"Something broke it," Al finally said. "Got into the cupboards looking for food. Something small we figured."

"Probably an oversized pack rat stocking up on supplies before this storm hit," Larry said with a chuckle. "Boy, the way it's coming down out there it should make for a grand opener. Those bucks along the swamp ought to be bunched up in there like spawning salmon." He looked at the boys and bobbed his eyebrows.

"Uncle Larry, this is my friend, Corey Stiles."

Larry stepped over and extended a hand to Corey.

"Uncle Larry is a park interpreter at Pictured Rocks for the National Park Service. He's a geologist. Leads groups of tourists along Lake Superior. Served two tours in Vietnam too. Was a kick-butt Ranger in the Marines."

The brightness in Larry's smile faded and his eyes lowered slightly.

"Come on, Brad," he said as he wrapped his big paw around Corey's hand. "Let's forget that kind of stuff in camp. We're all just deer hunters here. Right?"

Larry's fingers enveloped Corey's hand like a baseball mitt. Corey managed a faint smile then withdrew his hand, wiping his palm on his pants.

Larry turned back to the stove. He held his hands over the flat iron top and rubbed his palms together. His eyes gazed at nothing in particular as he stood in silence.

Brad watched him. There he goes, withdrawing into that part he doesn't want anybody to know. Crap, must have been my big mouth again that sent him there. I know Uncle Larry doesn't like talking much about the past, the war. But it's all so exciting. Figure he's got to have a ton of cool stories about it. Why does it bother him so much? What happened then? Oh well, I know what he does like to talk about anyway.

"Why don't you show Corey your gun, Uncle Larry."

Larry turned slightly and paused. He finally blinked, his eyes focusing again, the ghost of a smile returning.

"Sure. Sure, Brad. Got it right here in the case."

From the long leather case fringed with buckskin, Larry withdrew a wooden longbow. He placed the lower end on the instep of his foot, and with a quick push-pull of his hands, bent the bow and slipped the bowstring into place. He plucked the string as he handed the bow to Corey. It was still humming a musical note when Corey gently took the bow.

"Man, I've never seen anything like this. It looks like something from a Robin Hood movie," he said, his eyebrows jumping high enough to touch the red hair draping his forehead. "Where in the world did you get it, an archery museum?"

Larry grinned.

"No, Corey, I made it."

"You really made this thing?"

"Sure. Used a piece of osage orange, hedge apple some people call it. The settlers used to plant it for hedge rows. Makes great bows. That rough side there is backed with deer sinew from leg tendons. The tips are made from the antlers of a buck I shot several years ago. That same deer provided the buckskin wrap on the handle and over the arrow plate. Even used his brains to tan the leather. Made the Flemish twist bowstring too, but I had to use Dacron, modern stuff. Sinew bowstrings don't last worth a darn. Even the Ojibways who lived up here centuries ago switched to more modern strings after the whites started trading in the north. But everything else on that bow is as primitive as the hills."

Corey's mouth hung open as he glided his fingertips up and down the bow. He held it toward the light, revealing the reddish-orange grain patterns along the limbs. He slowly shook his head.

"Man, this thing's awesome. Can you really kill something with this? I mean a deer or something big?"

Larry chuckled and tipped his head. "Sure can. I've taken deer with self-wood longbows like this for the past eleven years. This is a new one, a lucky one at that. I've been fortunate enough to harvest an 8-pointer and a bear with it so far this season. Lots of small game too. It's a sweet shooter."

"Fortunate, heck," Granddad said, stepping next to Larry. "This bear here hunts more like an Injun or a cougar than a man. Only white man I've even seen that could slip up on a sleeping deer and slit its throat if he wanted."

"Come on, Dad that's a bit much. You're starting to sound like Brad here. I'm just a little lucky, that's all."

"Horsefeathers," Granddad continued. "Don't let him soft-sell you Corey. He's a deer hunting fool, a predator from the old days."

He reached up and draped an arm around Larry's shoulder. Larry shrugged and smiled at his dad, suddenly looking like a shy boy.

"Well, I suppose we ought to be hitting the hay," Al said. "Daylight in the swamp will come mighty early tomorrow."

Crane stood from the couch and stretched. He rubbed his ample belly and yawned. Vern picked up his empty can from the floor and dropped it into the bag with the others.

"Larry's going to have to sleep on the sofa," he said, avoiding Larry's eyes and glancing toward the window. "That's the only empty spot in the cabin. He'll have to make do. This ain't a hotel."

Brad watched Larry withdraw again into himself, stepping back into a shadowed corner of his mind. Heck, Uncle Larry could make do out in the snow if he had to. Just because Vern owns half this place doesn't give him the right to be such a prick all the time. Why can't Dad at least stand up for his own brother? If I was Uncle Larry I'd break Vern in half, just for starters.

"Sofa will be just fine, thanks," Larry said after a moment. He cast Vern a empty look — no smile, no scowl, no nothing, just a blank wolf stare, a probing wild void that could mask any realm of emotion. Vern quickly looked away as if icy claws were reaching out for him. He turned toward the back bedroom.

"Like your dad said, Brad, daylight in the swamp comes early," Granddad said. "Off to bed with you boys. It's been a long day for you both and tomorrow will be even longer. Guarantee it. Opening day has a way of becoming one of the longest in your life. Now go on, scurry up in that loft like pine squirrels."

Brad and Corey climbed into the loft and crawled inside their sleeping bags. Their cots creaked as they squirmed inside their bags. Below, others settled into bedrooms.

"Your Uncle Larry is really cool," Corey whispered. "It's like he came from some other place and time. Like some guy right out of a mountain man movie."

"Yeah, he's one of kind alright. Hunts, traps and fishes most of the year. Lives alone in a cabin near the big lake. Always says he was born two hundred years too late."

"What are those little beads around his neck?"

Brad glanced through the rungs of the railing. "Indian beads of some kind," he said. "Uncle Larry's really into old Indian ways. Sometimes I wonder if Granddad didn't adopt him from an Indian tribe."

Corey raised up on his elbow.

"Lay back down, I'm just kidding. He's a loner that's all. I guess people who live alone seem a bit strange to the rest of us. Maybe that's why Vern doesn't like him. Too much of a lone wolf to be trusted. Who knows?"

"Well, I still think he's neater than hell," Corey said, burrowing into his bag.

Corey quickly drifted off, his breathing measured slowly against the faint ticking of the alarm clock under Brad's cot. Brad sighed and laced fingers behind his head. He stared at the ceiling. How can tomorrow be longer than today? Geez, building stickups, getting chased by that coon, getting lost, wading through all that snow.

He closed his eyes but sleep wouldn't come. The cabin grew quiet except for the hushed conversation of his dad and Larry still sitting near the stove. Brad's breathing began to slow. His muscles relaxed. The warmth of the bag started to draw him into the darkness of sleep. He faintly overheard his dad telling Larry about their incident with the coon. Larry's calm voice suddenly grew strained as he spoke words Brad didn't understand. Brad's ears prickled. His eyes flicked open.

"Matchi Manitou," Larry said, as if a icy hand had squeezed the words from his stomach.

"What?" Al asked.

Brad sat up and cocked his head.

"Matchi Manitou, the evil one. The Ojibways had other names for him, Winabijou and Manabozho. Each swamp held one, an evil spirit that dwells there for all time. You know the Indian legend of Deadman's Swamp. There's a reason so many hunters have vanished there over the years."

"And you think it's this Matchi whatever? Are you kidding?"

Brad cupped a hand to his ear.

Only a drawn silence filled the room below.

"Please, Larry," Al whispered. "You know how Vern gets all worked up over this Indian legend stuff. So let's keep this just between us. And for God sakes, with Brad's imagination, the last thing we need is to plant that seed in his mind. Let's just forget it, okay?"

"Yeah, sure," Larry replied. His voice distant.

Al stood and turned down the gas lamp. Larry unrolled his sleeping bag on the couch.

"What's the Indian meaning of this Manabozho thing," Al asked, curious in spite of himself.

"He's a bad one. Specializes in luring young hunters to their deaths; hunters trying to make their first kill to show they're worthy to become braves."

"How does it do that?"

"Manabozho is a shape-shifter."

Brad's eyes flicked wide as he suddenly recalled the strange shape in the swamp and the feeling that whatever it was out there somehow wanted him.

Al stood in silence as the gas lamp faded to a dull orange then flickered out. He turned and went to bed, the floor boards creaking under his weight like the grinding of old bones.

Dare to wade into the mystery and fear of Brad's ordeal by taking the ultimate deer hunting adventure. To order the other 33 chapters of ***Opening Day****, simply fill out the order form in the back of this collection, or call in your credit card order today. Besides being a great read for hunters, the insights into hunting in this book make it an ideal gift for the anti-hunter or uncommitted non-hunter on your list.*

Caution: *We do not recommend reading this book alone in hunting camp.*

HAVE YOU READ *TRADITIONAL BOWYERS OF AMERICA* by Dan Bertalan?

If you're interested in traditional bowhunting, this book is for you!

In profiling 30 of America's top traditional bowyers, this hefty volume reveals over 700 cumulative years of bowhunting and bowmaking adventures. It details the building of recurves and longbows, offers valuable advice on selecting the perfect custom bow for you, tells how to improve your instinctive shooting, gives big game hunting tips from east to west, and serves up a potpourri of exciting bowhunting stories.

Just listen to what the experts say about this book.

"This book is so entertaining, so informative, I read it from cover to cover two times before I could get back to work! I find it to be a much used reference in my day-to-day work. The amount of history in this book cannot be found anywhere else, and no bowhunter should be without it in his or her own personal library." *T.J. Conrads, Editor/Publisher, Traditional Bowhunter magazine.*

"It's an excellent book for hunters who are considering a switch to longbows and recurves from compounds. It offers knowledge that can't be obtained anywhere else." *Dave Richey, Outdoor Editor, The Detroit News.*

"This is a must read for anyone interested in the heritage of American archery and hunting." *Dwight Schuh, Author, Bowhunting Editor for Sports Afield magazine*

"I missed two days of hunting because I got so engrossed in reading *Traditional Bowyers of America*...real down to earth style of writing...I felt I was sitting in those bowyer shops...my latent desire to build a longbow has been rekindled." *Vern Struble, Professional Bowhunter's Society Librarian.*

"The most interesting, entertaining, book I've read in years. A timely text of the life-styles and/or philosophy of some of the greatest men in our sport...the roots and seeds of bowhunting...yesterday, today and tomorrow." *Gene Wensel, Bowhunting Author and Outdoor Writer.*

Traditional Bowyers of America :528 pages, 166 photos, glossary, index, hard-cover.

What more can we say? If you're a traditional bowhunter, you owe it to yourself to buy this book, today! Credit card orders accepted. Call now, 517-834-2276. Or send check or money order to; Envisage Unlimited Press, P.O. Box 777, East Lansing, MI 48826-0777. $29.95 plus $2 shipping (MI residents add $1.20 tax).

IF YOU THINK YOU'RE READY FOR THE DEEP WOODS, WE DARE YOU TO TAKE THE ULTIMATE DEER HUNTING ADVENTURE...

THE YOUNG HUNTER — Fighting the uncertainties of buck fever and forces that defy definition, he struggles to discover the emerging man and hunter within.

THE FATHER — Suddenly cast into a gauntlet of survival, he claws past the trappings of modern man into the well of hunting heritage in an attempt to save all he loves.

THE GRANDFATHER — Once a hunting legend, now forced to face the limits of age, using his one remaining skill to possibly survive.

THE UNCLE — Possessed by a haunted past or Indian spirits? Or keeper of Deadman's Swamp's darkest secret?

THE HUNTERS — Mutations of man? Or ancient spirits destined to claim the souls of two-legged hunters?

Dare to become part of the mystery and horror of the Mercer hunting camp as the runaway forces of nature and circumstance cast them into a deadly spiral of survival.

Besides being a great read for hunters, the insights into hunting in this book make it an ideal gift for the anti-hunter or uncommitted non-hunter on your list. Change someone's attitude about hunting today by sending them a copy.

CAUTION! We do not recommend reading this book alone in hunting camp.

"Betcha you can't read just one page of Dan Bertalan's ***Opening Day.*** *This is a swift-running page-turner that is part science fiction and part Stephen King, yet pauses just long enough to reflect on the instincts and values inherent to modern-day hunting."* Patrick Durkin, Editor, Deer & Deer Hunting magazine.

"Combines the lyrical beauty of the Michigan North woods with a fascinating look at the predator hidden deep in all of us. Even as a non-hunter, I found ***Opening Day*** *full of hard truths and compelling logic. Makes the best case yet for the role of the caring hunter in the preservation of wildlife."* Mark Woodbury, Writer, Environmentalist.

OPENING DAY... The day you wish you hadn't gone into the woods.

256 pages, softcover, only $11.95 *(plus $2 shipping)*

Call in your credit card order today, 517-834-2276. Or, send check or money order to: Envisage Unlimited Press, P.O. Box 777, East Lansing, MI 48826-0777.

ABOUT THE AUTHOR

A national award winning outdoor writer, Dan Bertalan's bowhunting articles appear regularly in *Bowhunter, Bowhunting World, Traditional Bowhunter,* and *Deer & Deer Hunting* magazines. His popular non-fiction books, *Traditional Bowyers Of America* and *Bowhunting's Whitetail Masters* have earned him international acclaim. With over 50 feature articles published in recent years, he is recognized as one of today's top bowhunting writers.

Exclusively a bowhunter, Dan has hunted across North America for 30 years, from the eastern barrens of Newfoundland to the western slopes of the Alaskan Peninsula, and from the far reaches of the Northwest Territories to the cactus flats near the Mexican border — and through it all, harvesting a dozen different big game species, many registered in the Pope & Young Club's record book.

An active supporter of quality, ethical bowhunting, he is a Regular Member of the Professional Bowhunter's Society, an Associate Member of the Pope & Young Club, a member of the NRA, a member of the Michigan Bow Hunters, and a member of Michigan Traditional Bowhunters. In the writing arena, he is a member of the Michigan Outdoor Writers Association and the Outdoor Writers Association of America.

He lives in rural central Michigan where he loves chasing whitetails and sharing his bowhunting adventures through writing — both real and fiction, from the heart and from the well of imagination.